THE 13th HORSEMAN

BARRY HUTCHISON

An Afterworlds novel

HarperCollins *Children's Books*

First published in Great Britain by HarperCollins Children's Books 2012
HarperCollins Children's Books is a division of HarperCollinsPublishers Ltd,
77-85 Fulham Palace Road, Hammersmith, London W6 8JB

The HarperCollins Children's Books website address is
www.harpercollins.co.uk

3

Text copyright © Barry Hutchison 2012

The author asserts the moral right to be identified as the author of this work.

ISBN: 978-0-00-744089-4

Printed and bound in England by
Clays Ltd, St Ives plc

For Kyle and Mia, my own little harbingers of doom.

And I looked, and behold a pale horse: and his name that sat on him was Death, and Hell followed with him.

–Revelations 6:8

PROLOGUE

THE VAST, LONELY wastelands of oblivion stretch out in all directions, infinite in their scale and in their emptiness. Darkness lies heavy over this most desolate of plains, like a burial shroud on a long-forgotten corpse.

This place – if, indeed, it can be called a place – has been this way since before the dawn of time itself. Uninhabited. Undisturbed. It will soon change. Everything will soon change.

Since the first fragments of reality came to exist, there has been nothing but silence here. Yet the silence in the air now hangs ominous and foreboding, as if the very cosmos itself is holding its breath, and waiting.

But waiting for what?

Like the leathery wings of a startled bat, the darkness

rustles. In time – though it is impossible to say how much – the sound swells in volume, until it crashes and thunders like a storm called down by the devil himself. In all the endless reaches of this place, there is nothing and no one to bear witness to this terrible sound. At least, not yet.

But soon a fragment of the darkness warps and buckles, contorting as if pulled by some violent, invisible hand. The shadows stretch like treacle, screeching and howling in protest as they are forcibly rearranged into a new form. A form that could almost pass for that of a man.

Almost.

Angry tendrils of inky black hiss and slither across his frame. A fabric woven from the dead of night crawls across bare, bleached bone: a living cape concealing his full horror from all the worlds.

Though freshly born, he is already aware of his purpose. He knows beyond question the reason for his creation. And he knows what he must do.

His empty eye sockets turn and fix on some unseen horizon. He has an epic journey ahead of him. He has unimaginable distances to cross.

It will not take him long.

CHAPTER ONE

DRAKE KNEW IT wasn't the frogs' fault. It couldn't be. They were, after all, only frogs.

And yet, if it hadn't been for them, he wouldn't be here now, standing before a jungle of tall grass and weeds, holding the smooth wooden handle of an ancient lawn mower. Then again, if it hadn't been for *him*, the frogs would never have exploded, his science teacher, Miss Pimkin, would still have her hair, and the top two floors of his school would still be where they were supposed to be. All things considered, he'd probably come off best.

He'd been marched to the headmaster's office before the dust had settled. By the time the fire brigade had finished beating Miss Pimkin's flames out, he'd been expelled. And all because he'd tried to help those frogs. So much for good deeds.

Moving school had been bad enough, but the only school he could move to was twenty-five kilometres away, and that meant moving house too. His mum hadn't been happy about that, and he'd been trying to make it up to her ever since.

The grass was the latest attempt. He'd promised he'd cut it the day they moved in. That was four days ago, and it was still standing as tall as ever. After a night spent lying awake, worrying about his first day at the new school, Drake had got out of bed at six-thirty, and decided the grass's time had come.

The back garden was fairly small – about the length of an average-sized bus. That was the good news.

The bad news was that the previous occupants didn't seem to have ever set foot in it, much less made any attempt to keep the grass in check. A tangled wilderness swayed gently in the summer breeze. Two-metre-high weeds waved slowly forward and back as if beckoning him in.

"OK," he said below his breath. "Here goes."

By the fifth push, Drake realised that the lawn mower was not doing what lawn mowers were meant to do. He knew that the purpose of a lawn mower – the entire reason for the existence of lawn mowers – was to cut grass. No one, it seemed, had bothered to tell that to *this* lawn mower.

It was an ancient, weather-beaten contraption, with five blades set into a barrel shape, so they spun as the mower was rolled forward. Or, at least, that was the theory. But the entire mechanism had rusted solid, meaning the blades remained completely motionless as Drake shoved the thing further into the jungle of grass. The effect was that he wasn't cutting the grass so much as temporarily flattening it down, only for it to spring back up the moment he'd passed, none the worse for its ordeal.

Still, he refused to go back into the house without having made some progress, so he tightened his grip on the handle, dug his toes into the soft ground, and pushed on until he was swallowed by the overgrown undergrowth.

His arms and shoulders quickly began to ache from the strain. Tiny insects with enormous appetites dive-bombed him, tormenting him with their teeth. Clenching his jaw, he heaved the lawn mower another half-metre up the garden, briefly pushing over yet another patch of head-high grass.

And then, without warning, the weeds parted and Drake and the lawn mower emerged into a neatly kept clearing. The grass beneath his feet was a deep, lush green – not the wishy-washy grey of the other stuff – and just a centimetre or so long. It looked like a putting green at a golf course, cut into a pattern of perfect straight lines.

A raised flower bed stood off to one side of the circular space, sprouting with all the colours of the rainbow. A single bee bumbled lazily from flower to flower, happily checking for pollen, and appearing not in the least bit bothered when it found none. Nearby, birds sang songs of joy and harmony to one another, and to anyone else who cared to listen.

But Drake noticed none of these things. Instead, what he noticed was the shed.

It stood in the centre of the clearing. Or perhaps *slouched* would have been a more appropriate word, considering its condition.

The shed was about two metres wide by three long, with a door taking up most of one of the narrow ends. The walls were a smooth, dark timber that appeared to be immune to the early morning sunlight. Shadows hung over the planks like camouflage netting. Contrasting with the cheerful brightness of the clearing, though, the effect was exactly the opposite of camouflage: the shed stood out like a big square sore thumb.

With a little red roof.

A cool breeze blew at Drake's back as he stepped away from the lawn mower and further into the clearing. Turning, he looked back at the house. He had an unobstructed view of his bedroom window from here, which meant he should've been able to see this place from up there too.

And yet, he hadn't. He hadn't noticed the neatly cropped circle. He hadn't spotted the shed. All he'd seen was grass and weeds and hours of thankless hard work.

"There's an explanation," he told himself quietly. "No idea what it is, but there's an explanation. There's always an explanation."

Drake believed most things could be explained. He knew ghosts were tricks of the light, and UFOs were usually helicopters, or balloons, or far too much alcohol. He knew there was an explanation for this too. And he knew where he'd find it.

He hadn't noticed the birds tweeting or the bees buzzing, so Drake didn't notice both fall silent as he approached the shed door. Nor did he hear the breeze hold its breath, or see the flower heads twist slowly in his direction as he turned the handle, eased the door open, and quietly stepped inside.

CHAPTER TWO

DRAKE STOOD IN the doorway, still gripping the handle, a scream trapped in a bubble at the back of his throat. He had expected the shed to be empty.

He had, as it transpired, been wrong.

A monstrous figure of a man sat on a folding deckchair directly in front of Drake, his broad, muscular frame making the chair look ridiculously small by comparison. Even sitting down, the man was a clear two feet taller than Drake, with a wild, flame-red beard that covered the bottom half of his face and reached almost all the way down to the floor.

His hair was the same colour as his beard, thinning on top, but long at the back and sides. It hung down over his bronzed shoulders, finally stopping around halfway down his back.

A scar ran from the top of his forehead to his cheek, passing through a milky white eye along the way. In one enormous fist he clutched a small red cylinder. It rattled noisily as he shook it back and forth. The clatter seemed deafening in the otherwise soundless shed.

There was a telephone mounted on the wall behind the man, thick with dust. It was an old-fashioned-looking thing, the type that had a dial instead of buttons. Only this phone didn't even have the dial part. It looked like a phone designed solely for receiving calls, and not making them.

The man didn't look up when Drake entered, just kept rattling the container in his hand, his eyes fixed on the table before him.

It was only as Drake spotted the table that he noticed the other men sitting round it. Afterwards, he would ask himself how he could possibly have missed them. Or one of them, at least.

The... *thing* sitting across from the first man appeared, at best, *vaguely* human. Or rather, he looked *exactly* like a small group of humans would look, were they blended together into a puree, then fed to another particularly hungry human.

Rolls of flab hung off him like tinsel from a Christmas tree. They drooped from his chins and from his neck. They hung down over the elasticated waistband of his grey jogging trousers. They bulged beneath his matching grey top and spilled out through splits in the reinforced seams.

The whole gelatinous mound of blubber wobbled as the man turned to look at the new arrival. He looked Drake up and down, then crammed an entire chocolate bar into his cavernous mouth. Sideways.

There was a wet smacking sound as the fat man's purple tongue licked hungrily across his lips, and then he spoke. "You must be the new fella," he said, in a voice like a turkey's gobble. "Thought you'd be taller."

"And I bet he thought you'd be less revolting," snapped the third figure, whom Drake hadn't even looked at thus far. He turned to look at him now, and was relieved to discover he appeared almost completely normal, aside from the white paper mask he wore over his nose and mouth, and the latex rubber gloves on each hand.

Reaching into the top pocket of his pristine white coat, the third man pulled out a pair of glasses. His eyes seemed to double in size as he positioned the spectacles on his nose. "Oooh, he's right, though," the man said, looking Drake up and down. "You *are* a shorty. Still, you know what they say. Size isn't everything!" The man snorted out a laugh. "No, but seriously. Don't worry about it, it's fine. Fine. You're perfect just as you are. Gorgeous."

"You sitting down then?" asked the human blancmange. He was munching on another chocolate bar, not even bothering to remove the wrapper first.

Drake's gaze shifted across each of the men in turn. The only sound in the shed was the slow, rhythmic rattling of the container in the bearded man's hand.

"Um... um..." Drake stammered. "Sit... sit down?"

"Well, you might as well!" chirped the third man, removing his glasses and slipping them back in his pocket. "I mean, let's face it, you *are* going to be stuck here for ever, after all!"

The door gave a loud *thud* as it swung closed. The three occupants of the shed listened to the boy's screams as he raced from the clearing and back towards the house.

"Oh dear," said the third man. "Was it something I said, d'you think?"

It was the man in the deckchair's turn to speak. He spoke with a broad Scottish brogue, his voice louder than the others', despite the muffling effect of his beard. "Oh, don't you worry. He'll be back."

"You sure?"

"Aye. I'm sure."

Without another word, he opened his hand, letting a small square object tumble on to the tabletop. All three men peered down at the markings etched on to the object's surface, and considered their significance.

"A four!" gurgled the fat man triumphantly. "War's got a four!"

"Aye, all right," sighed the one known as War.

"Down the snake you go!"

"I can see that, thank you, Famine. No need to rub it in."

"Right then, Pestilence, my old son, your shot," said Famine to the man in the white coat. He rubbed his sweaty hands together excitedly. "And pass me them chicken legs, will you? I am bloody *starving*!"

✛

"Mum! Mum! There's nutters in the garden!"

Drake scrambled through the grass towards the house, leaving the clearing, the shed and the three strange men behind. The weeds and bracken whipped and scratched at him, but they didn't slow him down. In no time, he'd made it through the jungle, barged open the front door, and bolted inside.

His mum was in the kitchen, rummaging around in her handbag and patting down her pockets.

She was dressed for work – black nylon trousers with faded knees, off-white T-shirt and pale blue tabard. She worked three cleaning jobs, spread out across the day so she was out more often than she was home. Now that they'd moved, she had longer to travel to get to work, so she was out even more than she used to be.

"Keys," she said. "Have you seen my keys?"

"Nutters," Drake panted, pressing his back against the door to keep it closed. "Three nutters. In the shed."

"What shed? We haven't got a shed."

Drake nodded, still getting his breath back. "We do," he said. "It's at the bottom of the garden. Didn't see it at first, but then I found it, and there are three men inside, and they might be dangerous, and—"

"Who's dangerous? What are you on about?" his mum asked. She was still hunting for her keys, only half-listening.

"The three men," he said again, less frantically this time. "In the shed."

"We don't have a shed," Mum said, before her face brightened as she lifted a tea towel off the table. "There they are – no wonder I couldn't find them."

She slipped the keys into the front pocket of her tabard. "Right, sorry," she said, finally giving him her full attention. "What's all this about a shed?"

✧

For ten minutes they had hunted through the grass, sticking close together as they searched for the shed. They had found nothing, aside from the lawn mower. It stood silent and still in a particularly dense patch of foliage. The clearing Drake had pushed the thing into was nowhere to be seen, and nor was the shed.

Over the course of the ten minutes, Drake's mum had become increasingly irritated. Finally, she'd told him off for wasting her time, and stomped back towards the house, muttering about missing her bus.

Drake followed his mum back into the house. He wanted to argue, but he knew there was no point. He had been sent to a child psychologist after the incident with the frogs, and if he kept going on about the shed, Drake had a feeling he'd be back there by the end of the week. He'd already begun the process of convincing himself the whole frog thing had never actually happened. Maybe, if he tried hard enough, he could do the same with the shed.

Mum looked at her watch. "Right, I'm going to head for this next bus."

"Will you be home after school?"

"What's today? Monday? Yeah, I'll be here for a bit, then I'm out again. Unless I get held up, but there's stuff to eat in the freezer."

Drake scraped together one more spoonful of cereal, and took a final glance out through the window at the back garden. Still no shed. "Right," he said at last.

"Go and get ready," she said, kissing him on the top of the head on her way to the door. "You do *not* want to be late for your first day at school."

CHAPTER THREE

"Well then, Mr Finn," droned Dr Black, his mouth pulled into a mirthless grin. "Perhaps you would care to fascinate and bedazzle us all by sharing something about yourself?"

The old teacher's leather seat creaked softly as he bent his skeletal frame forward and leaned his elbows on the neat desk. "Aside from your apparent inability to arrive at my class on time," he added, "which we are all now only too aware of."

Dr Black was the most angular person Drake had ever seen. Every part of him seemed to taper to a sharp edge, from his pointed chin to the cheekbones that jutted like tiny pyramids from the craggy desert of his face. He wore a dark, neatly pressed suit that looked a size too big for his spindly body. His fingers, which he was steepling together in front of him, resembled chicken bones with fingernails drawn on the ends.

Drake turned from Dr Black's gaze and swallowed nervously. His new classmates sat like a battalion before him, row after regimented row of unfamiliar faces watching him expectantly. He felt his mouth go dry as his mind frantically scrambled to dig up just one interesting fact to share. All he needed to do was come up with a piece of trivia about himself that was so interesting they'd all be clamouring to become his friend. The only problem was that right now he was having difficulty remembering his own name.

He could tell them about the shed this morning. But no, that would make him sound insane. What could he tell them, then?

Drake felt a tickle as a bead of sweat formed just above his nose. It meandered all the way down to the tip, before dripping silently on to the scuffed floor.

"Mr Finn?"

"I had Frosties for breakfast," Drake babbled. He bit down on his bottom lip immediately, trying too late to stop the words spilling out of his mouth. His eyes flitted between the six or seven stunned expressions in the front row, and for a few long moments the world seemed to stand perfectly still.

Three boys, shorter than all the others, began sniggering at the back of the class. Drake leaped into the air as the teacher slammed his hands down hard on his desk and roared "BE QUIET!" No one else sniggered after that.

"Well," said Dr Black, composing himself. "That was… enlightening." He unfolded upright and gave Drake a firm tap on the back of the head. "Now, if you could endeavour to contain your sugar high long enough to take a seat, the rest of you turn to page two hundred and forty-seven and we'll find out what the history books have to say about my old pal, Attila the Hun."

Drake sidestepped through a narrow corridor left between two rows of desks until he came to the only empty seat in the classroom. He hurriedly sat down, desperate to blend in and no longer be the centre of attention.

Almost at once, a skinny girl with big eyes and short hair leaned across from the next desk over and flashed him a smile. "Hi," she whispered.

"Um, hi," he whispered back.

"You shouldn't eat Frosties," she told him. "Do you have any idea what goes into those things?"

"Sugar and cornflakes?" Drake guessed. This seemed to

take the wind right out of the girl's sails.

"Right. Exactly," she agreed. "*And* they exploit tigers," she added, rallying somewhat.

"Yeah, but… cartoon tigers, though," offered Drake weakly.

"Still tigers, though, innit?" the girl continued.

"Er… I suppose so," Drake shrugged. He noticed a brief flicker of a smile pass across the girl's face. "Are you winding me up?" he asked.

"Might be," the girl admitted, and the smile widened further.

"Right. Who are you, by the way?" Drake whispered.

"Mel Monday," beamed Mel, holding out her hand for Drake to shake. "I'm your new best friend."

✦

It was around four hours later when Drake found himself hurrying through a twisting labyrinth of corridors, desperately hunting for the boys' toilets.

He'd spent the first fifteen minutes of the lunchtime break searching, and he almost yelped with delight when he finally spotted the familiar black outline of a man that signalled the end of his search.

He was hopping from foot to foot as he pushed through the door and into the overpowering, yet strangely comforting odour of the toilets. Drake's fingers fumbled with his trousers, finding it difficult to undo the safety pin that had held them up ever since his button broke off last term. The trousers were a size too small now, which only served to make the pain in his stomach ten times worse.

With a triumphant cry, he finally managed to get them undone. Drake let out a loud sigh of satisfaction as a morning's worth of pent-up terror sloshed past the lemon fragrance cubes and down the drainage hole of the stainless steel urinal wall.

He was barely halfway through when something hit him heavily on the back. He stumbled forward, spraying his trouser legs with urine. Powerless to stop mid-flow Drake twisted his neck and looked down into the greasy, gargoyle-like faces of the trio of shorter boys who'd been sniggering at him in Dr Black's class that morning. They scowled back up at him.

"You shouldn't have come here," said the raspy-voiced leader of the group, his eyes little more than narrow slits in his pock-marked cheeks. "These are *our* toilets. No knob 'eads allowed!"

CHAPTER FOUR

HE SLITHERS THROUGH the walls between worlds, crossing dimensions in the blink of an eye. How many planes of reality has he traversed? One thousand? Five? He has no idea, nor any desire to know. He knows where he is going, and he knows, in time, he will get there. That is enough.

The entirety of time and space surrounds him in all directions. He pays it no heed. Only one location matters. Only one destination is his goal.

Shed, he thinks, though he does not yet understand the word's meaning. *I am summoned to the shed.*

CHAPTER FIVE

Today, Drake was coming to realise, was not his day. First the three weirdos and their disappearing shed, now this.

"'Ere, knob 'ead," the lead bully spat, "had any more Frosties this morning?" "Not since breakfast," Drake said, over his shoulder.

The boy scowled. "Like Frosties, then, do you?"

"Yeah, they're all right."

"I bet you do. I bet you love 'em."

Drake hesitated. "What's that supposed to mean?"

"*Shut up, knob 'ead!*" barked another of the bullies.

"Yeah, shut it, *Frosties boy*," warned the third, smiling inwardly at his own comedy genius.

A near-silence followed. Drake's bladder continued to empty.

"Right, this is taking too long," the little group's little leader snarled. "Get him, lads!" He stepped aside to allow his two henchmen a clear run at Drake. Neither of them raced into action.

"I dunno, Bingo," said the larger of the two. "Don't you think we should wait? You know, until he's finished?"

"*What?*"

"I'd prefer it if you did," said Drake, glancing over his shoulder at the three tiny tyrants.

"Shut up, no one asked you!" snapped Bingo. "Go on," he barked, pushing his cohorts forward. "Get into him!"

"Spud's right, I don't want pee on me," said Dim, the third member of the gang. His dirty face frowned below a mass of greasy ginger hair. "My mum goes through the roof when I get pee on me."

"Right. OK. Fine," Bingo sighed, squeezing the bridge of his nose between finger and thumb. "Wait until he's finished, *then* get him. Happy?"

Spud and Dim seemed satisfied with this compromise. All four boys stood in silence, the only sound in the room the splashing of Drake's slowly draining bladder. Bingo muttered under his breath as he impatiently tapped his foot on the tiled floor.

"Can we hurry this up?" he spat. "We haven't got all day."

"Sorry," offered Drake, his gaze now fixed on the matter at hand. "I'm going as fast as I can, but I've been holding it in for a while. Maybe you could come back later?" he suggested hopefully.

"Nice try. Just get a move on."

Despite his calm exterior, Drake was fighting back a full-scale panic attack.

He hated violence, but he knew that as soon as he'd dripped his last drip into the urinal, he was almost certainly going to find himself on the receiving end of some. They didn't look like they could be reasoned with. He couldn't run away, and he didn't think an outburst of tears was going to win any sympathy with this lot.

There was nothing else for it. He could see only one way out of his predicament. Only one way to avoid a full-scale pummelling from half-scale bullies. It wasn't going to be dignified. It wouldn't be pretty. But it was the only option left.

Swallowing hard, Drake spun one hundred and eighty degrees and let rip.

"My mum's going to kill me!" screamed Dim, as the first

yellow splashes hit his white polo shirt. The other bullies had the sense to keep their mouths tightly closed as they staggered back into a toilet cubicle, their arms crossed in front of them to protect them from the spray.

"You're dead!" Bingo screeched, slamming the stall door closed. "You're so dead!"

His ammunition drained, Drake hurriedly did up his trousers and dashed for the door. Dim moved to grab him, then slid on the slippery floor and splashed down into the puddle at his feet. Drake's fingers had barely wrapped round the metal door handle when he heard the cubicle fly open behind him.

"Come back here!" Bingo bellowed, his spotty face a mask of pure rage. "I'm gonna *kill you*!"

Drake stumbled out into the corridor, and failed to notice his safety pin pinging open. He powered forward, so focused on escaping that he also failed to notice his trousers slipping down round his ankles. He staggered forward for a few frantic paces until, with a *clunk* and a *thud*, his head and upper body hit the ground, one after the other.

He was lying there, his cheek against the floor, the seat of his boxer shorts pointing towards the ceiling, when a pair of polished black shoes stepped into his field of view.

"Get back here, you knob 'ead!" demanded Bingo, as he and his gang burst from the toilets. "I'll make you wish you'd never been—" The bullies skidded to a halt mid-sentence, their eyes fixed on the figure before them.

"Mr Bing," droned Dr Black. "I should have known."

Drake rolled on to his back, bucking and twisting as he pulled his trousers up. He could see right up Dr Black's nose from where he was. For a moment he thought he could see a tiny blinking light inside the teacher's left nostril. Then he realised that wherever he looked right now he was seeing tiny blinking lights. The knock to the head must have taken more out of him than he'd thought.

"On this occasion," said Dr Black, lowering his gaze in Drake's direction, "I'm electing to believe you are solely the victim of this little encounter, and not the perpetrator. Should it happen again I will not be so certain. Understood?" Drake nodded quickly. "Good," the teacher said. He returned his gaze to the three bullies cowering before him. "You boys," he scowled. "My classroom. Now."

"Hey, Chief, where you been?" asked Mel, appearing behind Drake as if by magic. "I've been looking everywhere for you."

"Toilet," said Drake, hurriedly refastening the safety pin to his waistband.

"OK, so maybe I didn't look *everywhere*," Mel admitted. "You going for lunch?"

"Nah, not going to bother," Drake replied, as casually as he could manage. He'd love to be going for lunch, but his free school meals card hadn't been sorted out yet, and he'd forgotten to ask his mum for cash that morning.

"Very wise," said Mel. "I'm not even sure the stuff they serve in there is technically food."

They walked on in silence past three or four more classrooms. Drake considered telling Mel about the disappearing shed, but he had no idea how to bring the subject up without sounding like a maniac, so he didn't bother.

Dr Black's door was swinging closed as they strolled by. Drake caught a glimpse of Bingo, Dim and Spud being led through another door at the back of the room, then the classroom door shut all the way over, blocking them from view. Drake wondered what was going to happen to them as he and Mel made for the stairs.

When they reached the ground floor, Mel stopped in her tracks.

"Euw," she winced, holding her nose. "What's that smell?"

Drake's mind raced. How could he tell her he had half a pint of urine all over his trousers? She'd laugh at him, or maybe never speak to him again. He'd only known her for a few hours, but for some reason he found that last possibility particularly disturbing. He was about to make up some excuse when a sour stench filled his nostrils and made his head go light.

"That's disgusting!" he gasped, pulling the neck of his polo shirt up over his mouth and nose. "What *is* that?"

He suddenly became aware of movement on the floor behind him. Drake turned and looked down. A messy ball of hair and legs looked back up at him, its scruffy head tilted quizzically to one side. Flies buzzed round its flea-bitten ears, no doubt attracted by the overpowering stench that surrounded the animal's body like a cloud of toxic gas. It was a cat. An unpleasant one.

"Hey, look, what a little cutie!" exclaimed Mel, apparently ignoring the evidence being presented by her own two eyes.

"A cutie?" Drake said. "It looks like a big scabby rat."

The cat bared a dozen rotting teeth and let out a growl. The deep, rumbling sound didn't fit the animal, and Drake found himself glancing around to see if a big dog was standing nearby, throwing its voice.

"I think you hurt his feelings," Mel scolded. Holding her breath she reached down and felt round the cat's neck. Below the matted fur she found a collar. Attached to the collar was a small metal tag shaped like a fish. "Toxie," she read. "His name's Toxie."

"How appropriate," said Drake, his shirt still pulled up over his face. "Now let's go before we catch rabies or something."

"See ya, smelly," Mel said, standing up and saluting the animal. "You be good now."

Toxie padded round in a circle and watched Drake and Mel continue along the corridor. His green eyes remained fixed on them until they had disappeared through a set of double doors.

"Woof," he said at last, then he stretched, sniffed the air, and sloped off out into the afternoon sun.

CHAPTER SIX

"**W**ELL?" ASKED MUM, bobbing eagerly into the kitchen. She was wearing a different coloured tabard now – green, instead of blue. "How did it go?"

"OK," Drake said with a shrug. "Got lost a few times, but it was OK."

"Come across any magic sheds?"

Drake pinned his smile in place. Better to let his mum go on believing he'd made the encounter up than to be sent back to therapy.

"No interesting ones."

Mum laughed. "Make any friends?" She lifted her jacket from the back of a chair and draped it over her arm.

"Yeah, one."

"Well done! He got a name?"

Drake felt his cheeks flush red. He knew what was coming next. "*She*," he said. "Her name's Mel."

"*She?* Good grief, that was fast work!" Mum laughed. She threw her arms round Drake and pulled him in close. "First day there and he gets himself a girlfriend!"

"She's not my girlfriend," Drake insisted when his mum let him go again. "She's just... Actually, she's a bit... odd."

"Odd's good!" Mum beamed. "Is she pretty?"

"Mum!"

"Sorry," she laughed. "Now, listen, I have to get going. I'm on until half-nine, but the way these buses are it'll be after ten before I get home, so get yourself something from the freezer."

"Will do," he said.

"In fact, do you know what?" Mum began. She fished in her bag until she found her purse, then handed him over a tightly folded ten-pound note. "Get yourself a pizza or something."

Drake's eyes went as wide as two six-inch-deep pans. His stomach rumbled at the mention of the word. Those Frosties were just a hazy memory.

"Pizza? Can we afford that?"

"It's my boy's first day at his new school," smiled Mum. "We can't let something like that pass without celebration. The phone's still not on yet, so you'll have to go out for it."

"Not a problem," said Drake, tightening his grip round the money. "Can I go now?"

"You can go whenever you like," Mum said. "I'm just getting ready and I'm off, so I'll be out when you get back."

"OK. Thanks, Mum. See you later."

"See you later," Mum said. She kissed him on the cheek, and then he was out of the kitchen, through the hall, and pulling open the front door.

As he stepped outside, his foot caught on something on the front step. He tripped, stumbled and fell with a clatter on to the path. Holding the money tight, he rolled on to his back and lifted his head until he could see what he'd fallen over. His eyes met the eyes of a small, mangy cat.

Toxie sat on the step, wagging his tail in a very un-cat-like way.

"Oh, great," sighed Drake, "it's you."

Jumping up, Drake pulled the front door closed to stop the cat wandering inside and stinking the place out. He stared down at the cat. The cat stared up at him.

"Right, come on, get out," Drake said, pointing to the front gate. "You can't stay in here."

The cat didn't move.

"Out!" Drake barked, striding along the path and throwing the gate wide open. "Go chase a mouse or something!" He looked down at the cat's stubby legs and fragile body. "Or an ant, or whatever it is you little guys chase."

Toxie sniffed, crossed his front paws on the ground, and rested his head on them. His eyes peered up through a matted fringe of browny-black hair. Every line of his body suggested he had no intention of going anywhere.

"Right, then," Drake sighed. He took two large paces forward, then bent down and scooped the cat up. He held it at arm's length, his face turned away. The stench was almost unbearable. "I didn't want to do this, but you've forced my— Hey!"

With a sudden jerk of its head, the cat's rotten teeth clamped round the ten-pound note in Drake's hand. The animal's frail body twisted in Drake's grip, and then it was on the ground, the money still held in its mouth.

"Give that back!" Drake cried, as the cat scampered off

round the side of the house. Drake gave chase, squeezing past the bins and the cardboard boxes that filled the little alley leading from the front garden to the back.

With a rustle, the cat vanished into the long grass at the rear of the house. Drake plunged in after it. There was no way he was letting that cat run away with his pizza money.

He pushed through the tangle of weeds and bracken, calling out as he ran. "Get back here. Get back here now!"

Drake was halfway along the garden when the instinct to give chase abruptly faded. He *swished* to a stop in a particularly dense patch of jungle.

What was he doing? He'd come running into the garden alone. Running into the area where he'd seen the shed and the three strange men in it. He'd been so focused on catching the cat and getting his money back that he'd forgotten all about it.

He listened for the cat, but heard nothing. It had probably already left the garden. His money would be long gone.

Slowly, so as not to draw any more attention to himself, Drake turned round and made a move back towards his house. The weeds opened like a theatre curtain as he shoved his way through.

A chill breeze danced across his skin as he stepped into a neatly kept clearing. Toxie sat on the closely cropped lawn, his tail thumping happily on the grass, the ten-pound note still held in his mouth.

Behind the cat, the shed creaked ominously in the wind.

CHAPTER SEVEN

THE TALL GRASS and weeds whipped at Drake as he high-tailed it away from the clearing. His heart thudded in his chest like a bongo drum made of terror as he frantically tried to put as much distance between himself and the shed as he possibly could. Were the men still inside? More importantly, had they heard him? One thing was for certain: he wasn't sticking around to find out.

With a gasp he leaped from the grass, expecting to land on the uneven concrete of the back step. Instead his feet found themselves touching down once more on neatly cropped lawn. The shed stood before him, exactly as it had done a few moments ago. He'd gone round in a circle.

He turned and surged back into the jungle of weeds. How could he have been so stupid? He wouldn't let it happen again. Fixing his eyes on the house, Drake made a beeline straight for it.

A few moments later he spilled out into the clearing. Toxie gave a happy yelp as Drake skidded to a halt on the grass. This was wrong. This was all wrong! Trembling with panic, Drake spun on his heels and darted back towards the high weeds. The men in the shed could be wanted criminals for all he knew. Murderers. Possibly even cannibals, judging by the size of the fat one. He had to get away.

"Haw, pal, you're wasting your time," boomed a voice from behind him. Drake's stomach bunched into a tight knot of fear and he propelled himself into the head-high undergrowth, not daring to look back. The weeds seemed to work against him, tangling and grabbing at him as he ran.

When he emerged into the clearing for the fourth time it didn't come as any great surprise. His legs and arms ached, his hands and face were covered in insect bites – even breathing was proving painful. The way he felt right now, death would almost come as a relief.

"Told you," said the bearded giant who stood in the clearing. He was casually running a large brick along the length of an enormous sword, spraying the grass with little orange sparks. "Now, you can try running again, but you'll only end up back here, and I'm getting fed up of hanging around waiting for you to get that through your heid."

The man had looked big when he was sitting down in the shed, but out here he managed to make the rest of the world look small. Arms as thick as tree trunks bulged from his torso, which spread out like a brick wall on either side of the long, flowing beard. Rusted chain mail covered two telegraph pole legs. Boots that may have once been wild animals of some kind were pulled tight over feet large enough to make the very planet itself shake. He looked dangerous. And he was staring directly at Drake.

"Wh-who are you?" Drake stammered.

"To some I'm the living embodiment of cruelty and suffering, who will rain fire and fury down upon them come the Day of Judgement," the man said gruffly. "To others I'm a big bugger with a red horse. Just depends who you ask, really." With a flourish he flicked the sword around and slid it into a sheath slung across his back. He wiped his hands on his leather tunic, then extended one for Drake to shake. "But you can call me War."

Hesitantly, Drake reached out and shook War's hand. His

own fingers felt all too fragile in the giant's grasp.

"Drake," he said. "Drake Finn."

"Aye. I know."

The shed door flew open and the skinny man Drake had seen earlier stomped out. He shielded his dark, sunken eyes from the sun as he marched angrily across the lawn.

"He's done it again!" the man shrilled. "He's eaten my antiseptic cream! That's the fourth one this week. I'll never get this rash cleared up at this rate!"

"I was hungry," called a voice from inside the shed. The wooden doorframe groaned in protest as the fat man appeared and squeezed himself through. He inched slowly forward, supporting himself with two walking sticks.

"You're always hungry!" snapped the scrawnier figure. He folded his frail arms across his pigeon chest in the universal language of sulk.

"Yeah," the fat man mumbled, licking dollops of thick white cream from round his mouth, "and you've always got a rash."

"This is Pestilence," War explained, stabbing a thumb in the skinny man's direction. "The walking dustbin over there's Famine."

"Nice to see you again," gushed Pestilence.

"All right?" nodded Famine. "Don't suppose you've got any crisps on you?"

"I'd shake your hand, but you'd only catch something," Pestilence continued, laughing nervously. "Still, I don't suppose it matters really, what with you being—" War glowered at him, cutting him short.

"With me being what?" asked Drake.

"With you being... *so handsome*!" Pestilence gushed.

"Or some cakes?" asked Famine hopefully. "I could really go a Swiss Roll."

"To understand who *you* are, you need to know who we are," War explained. He bent forward slightly and glared down at Drake. "Do you know who we are?"

Drake's gaze swept across the expectant faces of all three men. None of them had made any move to kill him, but that didn't mean it wasn't coming. It'd probably be safer to play along with their game, then make a run for it the first chance he got.

"War, Pestilence and Famine," he mused. "Those are the Horsemen of the Apocalypse, aren't they?"

"You've studied your religious texts," said War approvingly.

"Actually, I saw it in a cartoon," Drake confessed.

"Oh."

"Even some mints would do! I'm not fussy."

"Sorry, I don't have any food," apologised Drake. Famine sighed and rubbed his swollen stomach sadly. "Hang on though, aren't there supposed to be four of you?" Drake asked.

"Aye, well... There *are* four of us," said War. There was a note of caution in his voice that couldn't be missed. "We're all here."

Drake frowned. Not only did these lunatics think they were mythological characters, they also couldn't count.

"No," he ventured. "There's three." He pointed at each of them in turn. "One, two, three."

"One," repeated War, pointing at himself. "Two." He pointed towards Pestilence, who gave a little wave. "Three." Famine's stomach rumbled as if on cue. "And four." The giant held out a finger in Drake's direction.

"Erm... what?"

"You're the fourth," War intoned.

"The fourth what?" asked Drake. He was stalling for time now, his eyes scanning for the easiest escape route in the weeds.

"The fourth Horseman of the Apocalypse," explained Pestilence.

"The rider of the pale horse," Famine chipped in.

"Death," announced War gravely. "You are the living personification of Death."

"Right," chirped Drake, after a pause. "Well, that's a turn-up for the books." He rested his hands on his hips and shook his head in wonder. "Death, eh? Who'd have thought it?"

"You're taking it very well," Pestilence told him. "I mean it must come as a bit of a shock, that. Finding out you're Death and everything."

"Not really," Drake shrugged. "I suppose it's just a case of – YOU'RE ALL A BUNCH OF NUTJOBS!"

With that he launched himself into the weeds once more, shouldering his way through them as quickly as he could manage.

"Mum!" he squealed as he crashed on through the grass. He wasn't even sure if she'd still be home, but he shouted for her anyway. "Mum, help, the nutters are back, the nutters are back!"

"She can't hear you, you know," War sighed, as Drake

stumbled back into the clearing. "We've... we've... What have we done again?"

"Created a reality loop," whispered Pestilence.

"We've created a reality loop in the garden," continued War. "Nothing gets in, nothing gets out. All roads lead right back to this shed. A bit of techno-magic mumbo jumbo the old Death put together for us before he packed up and went."

"Went? Went where?"

"Went mental," Famine snorted. He was munching on a hunk of beef. Drake didn't want to think about where he'd found it.

"That's enough, Famine," War warned. "He went away. Retired." War was choosing his words carefully. "To... pursue other projects."

"And you're the replacement!" beamed Pestilence. "You're our new leader!"

"I'm not the replacement anything!" Drake exclaimed, throwing his arms up in the air. "I'm not Death!"

"Course you are," Pestilence argued. "Think about it, even your name says you are. Drake Finn. D. F. Death."

"What? D. F? What's that? That doesn't sound like Death!" Drake protested. "It's *deaf*, if anything! What, the end of the world is going to be ushered in by the hard of hearing, is it?"

Something nudged gently against his ankle. Toxie sat by his foot, gazing happily up at him, his tail thudding out a regular beat on the ground.

"And I suppose this is my horse, is it?" Drake scoffed, as he bent down and took his money from the animal's mouth.

"Actually," said War, "he's a Hellhound, but he owed us one so he helped bring you here."

"A Hellhound?" Drake said, stuffing the note in his pocket.

"Aye."

"But... it's a cat."

The thudding of Toxie's tail stopped, and an uneasy silence descended on the clearing. Even Famine had paused, his food halfway to his open mouth.

Pestilence cleared his throat quietly. "I'm sure he didn't mean anything by it," he said, his eyes fixed on the scabby cat. "It's a lot for him to take in."

For a few long moments the world seemed to stand perfectly still. Then, with a low "Woof," Toxie turned and wandered off across the grass. All three men let out a quiet sigh of relief.

"Bit of advice," War scowled. "Don't go insulting a

Hellhound, particularly not one that's standing next to you at the time."

"But... it's a cat," Drake said, his voice a low whisper. "I wasn't insulting him, he's a cat!"

"He's got some problems. With changing," Pestilence said, mouthing the last two words silently. "Bless."

"Changing? What are you—?"

"It's not important," War intoned, his voice clipped by irritation. "You need to join us in the shed."

"No."

The giant frowned. "No?" he repeated, as if hearing the word for the first time in his life.

Drake's fear had temporarily deserted him, replaced instead by anger at being kept against his will. "You said I'm in charge here, right?"

"That's right," said War reluctantly. "Death is *technically* the leader of the Four Horsemen, but—"

"Then I order you to let me go. No garden looping or any of that. Put it back to normal and let me go home."

"But we haven't even started discussing your responsibilities," War protested. "There's a lot to get through if—"

"Now!" Drake demanded.

War's bulging muscles twitched briefly. He bit down on his lip, fighting the urge to shout. An icy shiver of terror shot down Drake's spine as he realised he may have gone too far.

Eventually, though, the giant gave a single nod of his head. "Whatever you say," he said. "Pest."

Pestilence reached into his pocket and pulled out what appeared to be a perfectly ordinary television remote control. He jabbed a few buttons, then slipped the device back in his pocket.

"You're free to go," said War.

Drake eyed the men closely as he backed towards the high grass. When he felt the foliage brushing against him, he turned and plunged off through the weeds. The others watched as the trodden undergrowth sprang back into place in his wake.

"Well," breathed Pestilence, "all in all I'd say that went really rather well!"

CHAPTER EIGHT

"SETTLE DOWN GUYS, settle down."

It was first period. Science. The teacher, Mr Franks, swaggered into the classroom, one hand shoved casually in his trouser pocket. In the other hand he carried a sheet of paper that he studied as he crossed to his desk. He half sat, half leaned on the table, facing the assembled class, still reading the note.

"Stop mucking about with that gas tap, Kara," he muttered, without looking up. "They're not for playing with."

Near the back of the class, Drake gazed absent-mindedly out of the window. The events at the shed yesterday evening were replaying over and over in his mind. He should have told his mum about the men again. She could have called the police and had all three of them arrested.

Then again, if she hadn't believed him, he'd be back at the child psychologist, and she'd be worried sick. Besides, she seemed so tired when she'd finally arrived home. He'd slipped off to bed without saying anything soon after that. And, he only now realised, he never did get that pizza.

He'd just have to stay out of the garden for a while, that was all. For ever, if possible. Life was complicated enough without a freak show trying to recruit him as their ringmaster.

Getting lost in the grass so many times had been weird, though. He was still convinced there was a perfectly rational explanation for it all. He just couldn't for the life of him figure out what it was. Still, it was bound to come to him eventually.

"Right, listen up, everyone," said Mr Franks. The low murmur of the class died down, as all eyes turned to the teacher.

"Billy Sharp, Michael Ash and James Bing didn't return home from school yesterday. The police are searching for them, but as of this morning I'm sorry to say they still haven't been found."

A low wave of chatter swelled across the room, sweeping from pupil to pupil as they turned to each other and began to guess what could have happened to their missing schoolmates.

"Can anyone remember seeing any of them after lunchtime yesterday?" Mr Franks continued. "If so, it's very important you let me know now." His gaze washed over the class. "Anyone?"

Drake watched the other pupils with interest. He had no idea who the three missing kids were, so he couldn't be of any help, but he hoped someone would know something. Their parents had to be worried sick.

"OK, then," said Mr Franks. "If any of you do remember anything, then let me or one of the other teachers know. Right away. I can't stress that enough."

He sat the paper down on his desk, then stood up straight. His eyes locked on to Drake and his mouth curved into a friendly smile.

"You must be Drake," he said.

"Um... yeah," Drake confirmed.

"Good to meet you. I'm Mr Franks, but everyone here knows my first name. Doesn't bother me. It's Darren, OK? Write that down if you want, so you remember. D-A-double-R-E-N. I'm not into that whole *teacher-pupil* thing. I like to think that we're all friends here, just sharing knowledge. That's all. We've all got knowledge and we're just sharing it around. Sound good?"

Drake nodded. "Um... OK."

"I thought it might," said the teacher, smiling broadly. "I'm quite new here too, so I know it can be a bit daunting." He looked around at the class. "But we're a pretty good bunch, I think. We won't see you stuck. If you need anything, just give me a shout."

"Thanks," Drake said.

"No bother," Mr Franks replied. He had just started to say "Right, let's crack on," when a knock at the door interrupted him.

"Come in."

The door opened slowly and a younger girl scurried a few paces into the class, then stopped, like a rabbit caught in headlights. Without a word, she thrust a note in Mr Franks's direction.

"Thank you," he said, taking it from her and reading it over. "You can go back to class," he told her, and she retreated gratefully into the corridor.

"Looks like you're already in demand, Drake," he said.

Drake blinked. "Um... what?"

"Dr Black wants to see you," the teacher said.

"He does? Why?"

"Doesn't say," Mr Franks replied. He looked down at the note again, in case he'd missed something. "Just says he wants to see you in his classroom as soon as possible."

Drake realised every eye in the room was trained on him. A summoning to Dr Black's classroom, he guessed, was not something that happened every day. A few rows away, he saw Mel looking back at him. She smiled encouragingly. For some reason, this made him even more nervous.

The legs of his chair scraped noisily in the sudden silence as he stood up.

"You'd better hurry," Mr Franks said, as Drake made for the door. "It's not a good idea to keep him waiting."

✦

Drake's footfalls echoed eerily along the empty corridor. He turned over and over in his hands the photocopied map of the school that Mr Franks had given him, trying to figure out where in the twisting black and white labyrinth he was supposed to be. But he was coming to the conclusion that the map was a complete waste of time. He folded it neatly in half, stuck it in his back pocket, and went off in search of anything that might look familiar.

Why did the history teacher want to see him? That was the thought that occupied him as he wandered through the bewildering maze of corridors and passageways. Was he in trouble? He hadn't done anything, so he didn't think so.

Unless those three bullies had said something about him peeing on them, of course.

He walked on, up a flight of stairs that he vaguely remembered from yesterday. He felt himself becoming more anxious with every step. It had to be about the incident in the toilets. Why else would Dr Black call for him.

Self-defence, that would be his argument. It was a desperate, last-ditch attempt at avoiding a beating, and he wouldn't, of course, even contemplate urinating on anyone again.

He stopped outside a gloss-painted door and read the little brass disc screwed into the wood. *D9*. This was the place.

Self-defence, he reminded himself, as he knocked once, then reached for the door handle. Dr Black would understand. He was probably a reasonable enough man, deep down.

Drake drew in a breath, assured himself there was nothing

to worry about, then pushed open the door.

He paused with the door half open and stared in wonder. A sphere, about the size of a large beach ball, lay on the floor. Its surface shone like polished chrome. Drake saw a distorted reflection of himself as he leaned in closer to get a better look.

SNIKT!

Two blades extended suddenly from hidden compartments within the ball. Drake leaped back, as the sphere rose into the air, and the blades began to spin.

✦

Drake's blood *pitter-pattered* on the scuffed vinyl floor in perfect time with his frantic footsteps. He sprinted along a corridor, trying desperately to escape the ball and its blades as they sliced through the air somewhere behind him.

He wiped his sleeve across a deep, bloody scratch on his cheek as he skidded round a corner and two-at-a-timed down a flight of stairs. The ball could easily outpace him on the straights, but it had to slow down for the bends, he'd quickly discovered. If he could find enough corners he could put some real distance between him and it.

"Help!" he tried for the fourth or fifth time. "Someone help me, please!" Once again, no one answered his plea. It was almost as if the school had been emptied of everything but the armoured sphere and himself.

Drake stumbled to a stop outside a classroom. Twisting the dull metal handle he shoved against the door with his shoulder, throwing it wide open. Staggering inside, he slammed the door shut again behind him, then turned to find something to block it with.

A strangled yelp of shock escaped his lips. Instead of a classroom, he found himself in a corridor. Not just any corridor, either. His trail of blood spots led directly up to the door he had just closed. Somehow he'd ended up back in the same corridor he'd just tried to escape from. How was that possible?

His mind raced back to the garden yesterday afternoon. A *reality loop*, they'd called it. And now it was happening again. They were trying to kill him. Those nutjobs were trying to kill him!

The next corridor swung into view as he flung himself round another corner. Drake felt his heart crash down to his toes. Ahead of him, the walls stretched out into infinity. He could hear the ball of death whizzing closer and closer, its spinning blades already stained with his blood. Pointlessly he powered forward, painfully aware that there was no way he could outrun the thing on a straight like this.

Within seconds the blades were biting at his back, their sharp teeth chewing up the fabric of his uniform.

He cried out in shock as the first blade scraped against his exposed skin. Instinctively, he threw himself to the ground. Death, he knew, would be on him soon.

A shadow fell over him. He heard the soft creak of leather and the gruff growl of a Scottish accent. "Stay down."

A sword flashed in a wide, horizontal arc across the corridor. With a screech of tearing metal, the blade passed through the ball, mid-flight. War crouched down, shielding Drake from the brief, blinding explosion. Shards of metal rained down around them, peppering the floor and walls.

When the debris had stopped falling, War stood up, his sword still held at the ready. The floating ball was no longer floating. Nor was it a ball. A tangled mound of wreckage lay on the floor, smouldering gently. War gave it a cautious poke with the tip of his sword.

"What... what was that thing?" Drake asked, using the

wall to pull himself to his feet.

War's eyes narrowed. "Techno-magic mumbo jumbo," he muttered.

"What, like—?"

"*Exactly* like that," War nodded. He looked along the corridor in both directions. "And exactly like them."

Drake made a noise that was embarrassingly like a whimper. Two more floating balls blocked each end of the corridor. Their blades spun to a high-pitched hum as they began to hover closer.

"Hold on," War commanded, scooping Drake up and depositing him on his back. Drake caught hold of the giant's armoured shoulders and clung on for dear life. "We're leaving."

"How?" Drake asked, his gaze flitting between the two spinning spheres. "There's no way out."

War's muscles tensed. He sprang towards the corridor wall, raising a leg. Plaster and brick exploded outwards as he kicked. "Aye, there is," he replied. The whine from the floating balls increased in pitch as they raced towards the hole in the wall. "Right then, sunshine," War warned, "whatever you do, *don't* let go."

CHAPTER NINE

DRAKE DUCKED, KEEPING his head behind War's as they crashed through the hole in the wall and out into the car park. War took two big paces, then jumped, clearing a waist-high wall with ease. The ground quaked when he touched down on the other side, and Drake had to kick frantically until he found a foothold on the giant's back.

War scanned the car park, his eyes flitting from vehicle to vehicle. Behind them, the floating spheres came in single file through the gap. Drake craned his neck to see them. They were back to moving slowly, creeping cautiously across the tarmac, weaving between the parked cars. Their blades spun, but they were hanging back, as if aware of the danger War posed.

"They're getting closer," Drake warned. "Shouldn't we be running? What are you doing?"

"Trying to remember where I parked," War muttered. His gaze swept across the rows of vehicles.

"What? You mean... you've got a car?"

War shrugged. The sharp movement almost made Drake lose his grip. "Not exactly," he said. He ran up the bonnet of the closest car and thudded on to the roof. The metal dented where his feet slammed down, and an alarm began to wail in complaint.

The school minibus was parked right next to the car. War raised his arms and placed his palms flat against the minibus roof. With a grunt of effort, he pulled them both up on to it.

"Aha!" he said, looking down. "There you are."

Drake heaved himself high enough to look over War's shoulder. A horse stood on the other side of the minibus. But a horse like none Drake had ever seen.

It was bigger than a normal horse, but that was only to be expected. War, after all, was bigger than a normal man. Much, much bigger.

The horse's skin was a bright, brilliant red, that shone like a ruby in the mid-morning sun. Its mane and tail were shades of orange and yellow. They danced like fire when the horse turned towards the minibus roof.

A worn leather saddle was slung across the horse's wide expanse of back. War leaped from the roof and landed expertly astride the saddle. The horse gave a loud *snort*, but otherwise didn't react to the sudden weight on its back. The spheres did react, though. They *swooshed* forward, suddenly appearing at either end of the minibus, their blades spinning into overdrive.

"Yah!" War roared, giving the horse's reins a flick. It sprang into action, clearing the next parked car from a standing start. The car behind it wasn't so lucky. Its roof caved in, shattering the windows and spraying glass in all directions.

The impact was too much for Drake. His grip slipped, and he found himself sliding down War's back. War shifted his weight forward, making room for Drake to land on the saddle.

"I told you not to let go," War said.

"Well... *sorry*."

"Don't do it again."

War's shoulder armour was held on by two thick leather straps. Drake caught hold of them just as the horse bounded forward again. It cleared the whole row of cars this time, landing on the road. The road surface cracked beneath its hooves, but there was no stopping it now. With another leap it cleared the low wall that surrounded the car park, and they were out on the open road, leaving the school behind.

Another alarm squealed. Drake looked back to see the spheres slicing through the air after them, their blades tearing through everything in their path. Four cars, five, fell apart like broken toys. The wall became bricks, the bricks became dust, and the balls of death were after them once again.

The horse galloped along the road, Drake's teeth rattling in his head with each thunderous footstep. The ground whizzed by, a speeding blur of grey. Up ahead, a car's rear lights flashed red as its brakes began to squeal. Drake caught a glimpse of the driver's wide eyes in the rear-view mirror, before the horse was leaping again, soaring over the car then resuming its run on the other side.

"That... that was *incredible*," Drake said.

"That? That was nothing," War told him. His beard was being blown backwards over his shoulder. Drake had to lean to the left to avoid swallowing the thing. As he shifted in the saddle, he saw the traffic lights looming ahead. They were on red. A steady stream of traffic flowed across the street just beyond them. War flicked the reins. "Watch this!"

Drake could see the faces of every passenger on the bus. They wore matching expressions of amazement as they watched the horse hurl itself into the sky. Its hooves skitted across the flat metal roof, showering the street with sparks. And then it was plunging back towards the ground, and Drake could feel his stomach being tossed up somewhere around his ears. The landing bounced him out of the saddle. He opened his mouth to scream, before War's hand wrapped round his ankle and pulled him back down.

"Thanks," he croaked.

"No bother."

The spheres sliced through the moving traffic, their blades puncturing the tyres and chewing the metal of every vehicle they passed. Horns blared, people screamed, more alarms joined in the chorus, but it was all just background noise to the clattering of the horse's hooves.

Drake turned in the saddle. "They're still coming!" he cried, though his voice was almost lost to the wind.

War nodded. "Aye."

"What do we do?"

A hesitation. "Can you ride?"

"What... you mean ride a horse?"

"Naw, a bike," War spat. "Aye, a horse."

Drake shook his head. "No."

"Well, that's just bloody marvellous," War muttered. "A horseman that cannae ride a horse."

"What? I can't hear you, it's too noisy!"

"Doesn't matter," War said more loudly. "Can you hold a rope?"

Brakes screeched behind them, followed by the *crunch* of metal colliding with other metal.

"What kind of question's that? Of course I can hold a rope."

War's hand reached back over his shoulder and plucked the boy from the saddle. Drake barely had time to realise what was happening before he was plonked down again. He recoiled in the force of the sudden wind. He was in front of War now, the big man's body no longer shielding him. A rein was pressed into Drake's hands. He heard the *shhnnk* of a sword being drawn from a sheath. "Good," War intoned. "Hold that, and for God's sake don't—"

The end of the sentence was lost as War rolled sideways

off the horse's back. He hit the ground shoulder-first, rolled on the tarmac, then sprang to his feet, his broadsword raised and ready.

Drake felt himself sliding in the saddle and clutched the reins tightly to his chest. "Don't what?" he cried. "Don't *what?*"

But War was too far away to hear. He stood his ground before the spinning orbs, eyes flitting from one to the other. They crisscrossed along the street, moving over, around and occasionally *through* the now stationary traffic.

"Ye want some?" the giant growled, twirling his sword round in his right hand. "Come get some."

The blades screamed through the air. One of the spheres raced ahead, closing in for the kill. War planted his size nineteens, put his weight on his front leg, and swung. The first ball exploded before the sword could connect. A hail of razor-sharp metal barbs burst forth. They rattled against War's armour and dug into the few exposed patches of his leathery skin.

He gave a low grunt as the hooks tore into his flesh, but followed through with his swing. The sword whistled through the space the first orb should've been occupying, then arced round in a full circle. He spun on the spot, bringing the blade back round, directly into the path of the second sphere.

The ball dipped sharply, dodging the sword and clattering against the ground beside War. He brought up a foot, slammed it down with a *ker-ack*, but the sphere was past him. It bounced twice, like a basketball, then spluttered back into the air. With blades whirring, it streaked off after the horse, and the boy on the horse's back.

"Aw," grimaced War. He pulled the first of the hooks from his arm and watched the ball rocketing away. "Bugger."

Drake bounced violently in the saddle, his knuckles white on the reins, his face fixed in a mask of terror. The horse's breath snorted in and out through its wide, flared nostrils, slow and steady, as if even this frenzied pace was taking no effort to maintain.

"Slow down!" he wailed. "Whoa! Stop! Whatever it is you do!"

Drake hadn't seen War's encounter with the armoured spheres, but that didn't matter. They were a distant memory now, a distant threat. The threat of falling off and splattering like an egg against the ground – that one was much more pressing.

The horse thundered on, muscles moving beneath its ruby flanks, its mane blazing like an inferno. They were almost at the end of the street now, surely moving far too fast to take the ninety-degree bend that was racing up to meet them. A row of shops lined the road dead ahead. Drake could see himself reflected in the glass fronts, four identical versions of himself on four identical horses, all about to be caught up in the same identical crash.

"Look. Building!" Drake cried, leaning down and shouting directly into the horse's ear. The ear flicked, as if swatting away a fly, but the horse's gallop didn't falter. "Come *on*," he begged. He bounced backwards in the saddle and gave a sharp yank on the reins. "We need to—"

With a whinny, the horse leaped into the air. Drake gripped with his legs and wrapped the reins round his wrist and braced himself for another jarring impact.

It never came.

"Stop," Drake whimpered, as the ground fell away and the horse's hooves began to clatter across the wide-open sky.

A long way back along the street, War plucked the last of the barbs from his skin as he watched his horse take to the air. Even there, a hundred or more metres away, he could hear the boy's panicked screams.

War shook his head. "I told him," he sighed, sliding his sword back into its sheath. "What did I tell him? For God's sake, *don't* pull back on the reins."

CHAPTER TEN

DON'T LOOK DOWN, don't look down, don't look down. The words repeated in Drake's head like a mantra. Looking down would be stupid. Looking down would be *insane*.

Drake looked down.

Aaaaaah, screamed his brain. *Aaaaaaaaaaaah!*

The town spread out below him like a map. The streets, the cars, the houses – they were all tiny, and getting tinier by the second as the horse climbed steadily higher.

The rushing of the headwind stole Drake's breath away. The horse's hooves *clip-clopped* noisily on thin air. Somewhere, far off to their left, a passenger on a passing aeroplane watched the horse running across the sky, took a long, hard look at his complimentary drink, then slowly sat it down on the fold-away tray.

And behind them, unnoticed, a spinning ball of techno-magic mumbo jumbo tore across the sky.

"D-down," Drake whimpered. "Down, boy."

The horse tossed its head back and shook its fiery mane. It banked steeply upwards, until it was almost running vertically. Drake screamed as he slid backwards off the saddle. The reins, still wrapped round his wrists, jerked tight and he found himself dangling helplessly, his legs bicycling in mid-air.

With a snort, the horse turned sharply right and began to race towards the distant ground. Drake was flicked upwards, before gravity thudded him back down into the saddle. He felt the upsurge of wind and heard the high-pitched whine of the sphere as it soared past him, tumbling end over end.

The ball curved like a boomerang, punched through a fluffy white cloud, then rejoined the chase. Up here, with nothing to get in its way, the ball was fast. It began to close the gap almost at once. Even over the roaring of the wind, Drake could hear the *whirring* of the blades. He remembered the sting of the cut on his cheek. Then he imagined it a thousand times worse.

He clenched his legs round the horse's broad back and ducked down low in the saddle. "Yah!" he cried, flicking the reins just as War had done. "Ya-*aaaaaaaaaaah!*"

The world went blurry round the edges. For the second time in sixty seconds, Drake was saved by the reins round his wrist as he was thrown backwards off the saddle. Still the horse galloped faster, until it was dragging Drake along, his legs stretched out behind him.

"Not *yah*," he cried. "I've changed my mind. Not yah! *Not yah!*"

The animal gave a long, loud whinny. It sounded, Drake thought, suspiciously like a laugh.

The roar of gunfire erupted behind them. The horse banked sharply to the right and something whistled past Drake's head. Several somethings. He glanced back and caught a glimpse of a gun barrel poking out from within the sphere.

"Yes *yah*. Definitely *yah*!" Drake cried. "Yah, yah, *yah*!"

Fire spat from the barrel of the gun. The horse went into freefall and Drake felt the bullets streak by just above him. He looked down to find the ground racing up. He'd barely begun to scream when the horse levelled off, clattering him back down into the saddle.

They were racing just a few metres above an open field now, kilometres outside the town. A road ran alongside them a kilometre or so to the left. Down on the right, a narrow river meandered towards an old stone bridge.

Twisting in the seat, Drake searched the sky. The ball was nowhere to be seen. "Where did it go? Did you see it?" he cried. He hesitated, then added, "Why am I asking a horse? I mean, it's not like you can understand what I'm saying." Another pause. "You can't understand what I'm saying, can you?"

The horse shook its head.

"Good," said Drake. "That would've just been too weir— *Look out!*"

The sphere rose up from behind the bridge, spraying bullets in a wide horizontal arc. The horse *neighed* loudly, startled by the gunfire. Stumbling, it plunged into the river. The coldness of the water made Drake gasp. It swirled in through his open mouth, filling his throat and his belly. He felt the reins pull away, heard the frantic splashing of the horse. And then he was floating.

And then he was sinking.

And then, he was drowning.

The darkness eased behind Drake's eyelids, like shadows fleeing the coming of dawn. Something warm and wet pressed against his mouth. And his cheeks. And his forehead. It pulled back as he sat up and spewed dirty river water on to the grass.

"Knew it," said Famine. His head was directly above Drake's, his rubbery lips folded into a wide smile. "Kiss of life. Never fails."

Drake turned his head and spewed again. Not water, this time.

"What... what happened?" he asked, when he had finished retching. "Where's the ball thing?"

"Over there." Pestilence's head appeared from behind Famine's bulk. He pointed to a scorched patch of ground nearby. "And over there. And there. And there's a bit down there, by those trees. War headbutted it. It was really quite impressive."

"You're lucky we found you when we did." War was standing a short distance away, running his hand over his horse's flank. "And you're lucky Famine's got his first-aid certificate."

"Have you been eating Frosties?" Famine asked. His tongue rummaged around inside his mouth. "You have, haven't you? That's definitely Frosties. And milk. Semi-skimmed."

Drake's hand went to his own mouth. "I think I'm going to puke again."

War clapped his horse on the back and turned to Drake. His face was beard, scowl and very little else in between.

"I warned you, didn't I?" he said. "'For God's sake,' I said, 'don't pull back on the reins.'"

"No, you didn't," Drake snapped. His pulse was racing, adrenalin pumping the blood through his veins. "You said 'For God's sake don't...' and then you jumped off. How was I to know the horse would start flying?"

"Don't be so stupid. It didn't fly," War said with a grunt. "Horses don't fly. They gallop."

"Well, it *galloped* across the sky!" Drake replied. He pulled himself up to his full, unimpressive height. "Horses don't *do* that."

"Well, that depends on the horse!" War roared, bending

until he was almost nose to nose with Drake. "Now, you're going to come back to the shed, and you're going to start your training."

"No, I'm not!"

War's face went the colour of his beard. He opened his mouth to shout, but Pestilence slipped between them and quickly guided Drake away.

"If I might interrupt," he said, smiling thinly. "I think what my irate colleague is trying to say is that we'd very much appreciate it if you'd perhaps come back to the shed and listen to what we have to say." He held up his hands. They were still hidden beneath white rubber gloves. "Just hear us out, that's all."

Drake remained silent for a long time. Pestilence watched him, eyebrows waggling encouragingly. "Here," Drake said at last. "Tell me here."

Pestilence glanced at the others, as if looking for some cue. None came, so he shrugged, then carried on.

"The Four Horsemen of the Apocalypse have existed since the dawn of time itself," he began. "We are servants of the Almighty, created for one purpose and one purpose only."

"To usher in the end of the world," blurted Famine.

"Oooh, shut up, you!" Pestilence gasped, his hands going to his hips. "I'm supposed to do that bit! You never let me do that bit!"

"Just get on with it," said War.

Pestilence shook his head. "That's my favourite bit," he muttered. "Anyway. Yes. We were created to usher in the end of the world." He looked pointedly at Famine before continuing. "It's a pretty important job, really. I mean, it's probably – what – sixth most important job in all creation?"

"'Bout sixth," Famine confirmed. "'Bout sixth, yeah."

"It's about the sixth most important job in all creation," Pestilence said. "And it's great. I mean, it's an honour to be picked and everything, it's just..."

Drake waited for the rest of the sentence. It didn't seem to be forthcoming. "It's just what?"

"God, it's dull," Pestilence groaned. "I mean, we've been kicking about for thousands of years, us three, just hanging around, you know? Waiting on the phone call. Thousands of years and nothing. Not even a false alarm."

"So? What's that got to do with me?"

"Death got fed up of waiting," Famine said. Drake could tell from the fat man's voice that he was munching on something. He couldn't bring himself to look and see what it was. "He decided he was going to bring on Armageddon himself and cleared off. Short of it is, we're down to three. And with him planning on destroying the world, the powers that be decided we needed a replacement, sharpish."

"You," said Pestilence.

"Me? Why me?"

Pestilence shrugged his slender shoulders. "No idea. We don't know the why-fors, we just know you're our fourth horseman."

"Fifth horseman, surely?" Drake corrected. "The last guy was the fourth."

Pestilence shot the others a nervous glance. Famine kept his own gaze on the ground. Even War looked slightly uncomfortable, but it was he who eventually broke the silence.

"Actually, he was more like the twelfth."

"Twelfth?" Drake said. "I don't understand."

"We've had... a number of Deaths," War admitted. "Nine, actually. Not counting you."

"*Nine?* Why? What happened to them?"

Famine crammed his food into his mouth and began

counting on his fingers. "Mad, mad, suicide, mad, quit, mad, goldfish, suicide, mad," he said.

"Wait," said Drake, replaying the list in his head. "Goldfish?"

"Admin error," explained Pestilence, rolling his eyes. "Do not even go there. You should've seen him trying to ride the horse."

"So, counting us three, there have been twelve horsemen before you," War continued. "Making you the thirteenth."

"Unlucky for some!" Pestilence trilled. He caught War's expression. "Sorry," he whispered. "Not helping."

"No, I'm not the thirteenth." Drake shook his head emphatically. "I'm not doing it."

"But it's a good job," said Pest encouragingly. "It's a *great* job!"

"*A great job?* They all killed themselves or went mad!" Drake cried. "That hardly screams 'job satisfaction', does it?"

"Well, no," admitted Pestilence. He held up a little red button with 'I AM 4' printed on it in jolly yellow lettering. "But you get a badge, look."

"Death Five didn't go mad or kill himself," Famine reminded him. "He quit."

"Right, well I'll do that, then," Drake said. "I quit. There."

War's voice was a low growl. "You can't quit. You haven't accepted the job yet."

"So, if I take the job, I can quit? Simple as that?"

"Aye. Simple as that."

Drake took a deep breath. "Then I accept. I'll take the job."

Pestilence clapped his hands. "Yay!"

"And now I quit." Drake turned and began to march off, towards where he hoped the town might possibly lie. "Good luck finding a replacement."

"Where d'you think you're going?" War demanded. The tone of his voice stopped Drake in his tracks.

"Home," he answered. "I told you, I quit."

"Fair enough," War said. "But you have to work your notice."

Drake met the giant's gaze and held it. "What?" he asked flatly.

"Three months' notice," War said. "Ninety days. It's in the terms and conditions."

"But..." Drake's mouth flapped open and closed. "You didn't tell me that!"

"Didn't I? Must've slipped my mind."

Over by the bridge, War's horse gave a snort. For the first time, Drake noticed a small shed standing just beyond it. It looked remarkably similar to the shed in his garden, but Drake decided he wasn't going to think about that right now. He had enough on his plate as it was.

"You don't want to go breaking the terms and conditions," War told him. "That's really not a good idea."

"Why?" Drake asked. He'd been running on pure adrenalin since his escapades on the horse, but the effects were wearing off now, and he could feel his whole body trembling. "What happens if I do?"

War's face darkened. "You'll be cast into the fiery pits of Hell for a thousand millennia, forced to endure torture and suffering far beyond anything your tiny little mind could ever bring itself to imagine."

"*And*," added Pestilence apologetically, "we'd have to take the badge back."

War folded his arms across his impossibly broad chest. "So, Drake Finn," he said, "what's it to be?"

CHAPTER ELEVEN

BY THE TIME Drake made it to town, his feet hurt. They were also damp. The rest of him had dried off during the long walk back, and the two hours spent hanging around near the school, waiting for the final bell to ring.

He knew he couldn't turn up at home before the end of the school day, or his mum would ask questions. Besides, the extra couple of hours had given him time to think, and to poke around the car park where he and War had made their escape.

Getting close proved impossible. Police had cordoned off the area where the wall had been smashed. They were combing over the remains of the minibus and the cars that had been trampled by the horse, or shredded by the spheres.

Drake had stared at the torn metal and the fragments of glass on the ground. Those blades, that could tear cars to ribbons, had been coming for *him*. He'd thought at first that the horsemen had sent them, but now he knew differently. But someone *had* been trying to kill him, and if it hadn't been the horsemen, then who had it been? And why?

These thoughts were still occupying him an hour later, when he stood at the front gates, waiting.

"Hey, Chief. Where you been?"

"Oh, um, hi," he said, giving Mel a self-conscious wave. "Didn't expect to see you here."

Mel heaved her bag higher on her shoulder. "What, exiting the school gates at bell time?" she asked. "Yeah, what are the chances?"

Drake's face suddenly felt very hot. "Yeah," he muttered. "Yeah, of course."

"No one's ever waited for me before," she said, matter-of-factly.

For some reason, Drake felt glad about that. "Really?" he asked, doing his best not to grin like an idiot.

"Most people think I'm strange." She looked at him intently. "Do you think I'm strange?"

"A bit," Drake admitted.

Mel brightened. "Excellent. I looked for you at break," she said. She started to walk away from the school and Drake fell into step beside her. "Where were you?"

For a moment, Drake thought about telling her the truth. But he didn't. The truth was too weird.

"I, uh, left early," he told her. "Doctor's appointment."

"Anything serious? You're not dying, are you?"

"Nah, just a check-up."

Mel whistled. "Must've been a long check-up. Break until now… that's, what, five hours?"

"Yeah. He was very… thorough."

"You missed some excitement," Mel said.

Drake's ears pricked up. "Oh?"

"There was a big accident in the car park. They're saying the school minibus crashed into the wall. Knocked a hole right through it."

"Who's saying?"

"You know… *they*," Mel explained. "Just they in general."

"Right," Drake said. "Wow."

"It's by *far* the coolest thing to ever happen in that school. Which is tragic, really, when you think about it. *Balloon!*"

Mel pointed excitedly up towards the sky. Drake followed her finger and saw a yellow balloon being carried on a breeze above the rooftops. "What's your stance on loose balloons?" Mel asked him.

Drake frowned. "Loose balloons?"

"As in *balloons that have got loose*. Like that one. What do you feel about it?"

"Um... not much."

Mel looked disappointed. "I'm in two minds," she said. "On the one hand, I think they're terrible, because it means that someone somewhere has lost their balloon, and that's got to sting, right?"

She looked at Drake expectantly.

"Right," he agreed.

"Right. But on the other hand, *it's a balloon*, so you've got to love it." She sighed. "I just don't know what to think."

Drake nodded. "It's difficult."

"That it is," she agreed. "That it is."

They watched the balloon until it disappeared into the fluffy white clouds. It looked, to Drake, impossibly high, and he tried not to think about the fact he'd been racing through those very clouds – or ones quite like them, anyway

– just a few hours ago.

"So, this accident," he said, as they continued walking, "what did you say caused it?"

"Well…" began Mel. She took a deep breath, and Drake got the feeling she was about to launch into a detailed account of what had happened. "They don't know," she said, proving him completely wrong.

"I thought you said it was the minibus?"

"No, *they* think the minibus crashed into the wall, but loads of other cars were damaged too, and the minibus couldn't have caused all of it."

"Oh, right."

"They even found horse droppings!" Mel said. "Can you imagine? Horse crap in the school car park? Picture it, Chief, a horse doing a great big poo right there on school grounds! *Just picture it.*"

"I'd rather not."

Mel shrugged. "Suit yourself."

"So no one saw anything… strange?"

"What, apart from the horse crap? No, don't think so."

So, no one had witnessed Drake's involvement in the destruction of the car park, or seen the flying spheres. That was a good thing, he decided. Probably.

"Why do you ask?"

"Um, no reason. Those boys turn up?" he asked, changing the subject.

"What? Oh, no, not yet. They will, though."

"How do you know?"

Mel puffed out her cheeks. "This is them all over. They'll have run away, but they'll come back when it starts raining or they run out of food or whatever. Everyone knows it, that's why no one's all that bothered about it." Her brow furrowed. "There was something else I was going to tell you."

"What?"

She looked up and to the left and right, as if she'd find the answer written there somewhere. "Nope, can't remember," she said at last. She stopped walking. "This is me."

Drake found himself looking up the long gravel drive of a grand detached house. Two cars stood in the driveway, both as big as his kitchen, both brand new. Drake made a mental note never to let Mel see where he lived.

"Wow, is this your house?" he asked.

"Yeah," she said matter-of-factly. "I'd invite you in, but my parents are Devil Worshippers."

"Really?"

"Nah. Well, my Dad's not."

A statue in the middle of the neatly cropped lawn caught Drake's eye. It stood twice as tall as him, reared up on its hind legs. "Hey, another horse."

"Oh, yeah, my whole family's into horses," Mel said, following his gaze. "I used to have one."

"What happened?"

Mel drew a thumb across her throat and made a sound like the snapping of bone.

"Oh, right," Drake mumbled. "Sorry."

Mel shrugged. "She was ill. It was her time. Horses die, and them's the facts." She looked at the house, then back to Drake. "So," she began, "see you tomorrow?"

"Assuming no more check-ups."

She smiled her crinkled-nose smile. "You look pretty fit to me," she said, then her face fell. "I mean... fit like *healthy*, not... you know? Though, I mean, not that you're not..." She pointed with a thumb towards her house and smiled lopsidedly. "I'm just going to go," she said, turning and crunching her way up the drive.

Drake watched her until she had disappeared inside the

house. Then he watched for a few seconds more, in case she came back out again.

When he was sure she wasn't going to, he turned and looked in both directions along the leafy street. "Right, then," he muttered, recognising nothing. "How the Hell do I get home?"

✦

Drake lowered himself on to the fourth seat. It had been pulled into place at the rickety table, between Famine and Pestilence, and directly across from War. The three men barely paid him any notice as he sat down. Their attention, instead, was fixed on War's hand. It crept slowly across the table, a short coil of red rope clutched between his trembling fingers.

"Careful," Pestilence whispered, then he clamped a rubber-gloved hand over his mouth to stop himself saying any more.

"Of course I'll be careful," War said through gritted teeth. "I'm *being* careful."

War took a deep, steadying breath, then he – *carefully* – hooked the rope in place. The Horsemen of the Apocalypse watched, none of them daring to speak a word until—

"*Buckaroo!*" cried Famine, as the plastic donkey kicked its back legs, showering the tabletop with a selection of brightly coloured bits of plastic.

"Bugger it," War muttered. He looked up and met Drake's withering gaze.

"You quite finished?" Drake asked.

"Aye, well, we are now," War said. "You here to start your training?"

"I don't know," Drake said. He leaned back in the chair. "I want you to explain it all to me first."

Pestilence cleared his throat. "Right, well, you see the donkey there?"

"Not Buckaroo," Drake said. "I meant explain..." He gestured around at the shed. "*Everything.*"

"I know," said Pestilence, smiling sheepishly. "Just my little joke." He began packing the game away into its battered box.

"Where do you want me to start?" War asked.

"Start at the beginning."

War shrugged, rolled his eyes and stroked his beard all at once. "Fair enough," he said. "In the beginning God created the heaven and the earth. And the earth was without form, and void; and darkness was upon the face of the deep. And the spirit of God moved upon the face of the waters."

Drake frowned. "What are you talking about?"

"And God said, 'Let there be light,' and there was light," War continued. "And God saw the light, that it was good: and God divided the light from the darkness."

"Right, stop, stop," Drake said. "What are you on about?"

"Genesis, chapter one," War replied. "You said to start from the beginning. Want me to keep going?"

"Is that the Bible?"

"Aye," said War flatly. "That's the Bible."

"Well, what are you telling me that for?" Drake asked.

"Because we're Biblical characters," War said. "You said 'start at the beginning', so I was starting at the beginning."

Drake snorted. "Biblical characters? Come off it. The stuff in the Bible's not real."

There was silence in the shed. Drake looked round at three equally reproachful expressions. "It's not, is it?" he asked weakly.

"Of course it's real," War growled. "It's all true. Well," he added hastily, "some of the translation didn't work out too well, but most of it's close enough."

"What... Noah's ark, the Ten Commandments, all that stuff actually happened?"

"Well, there are only four commandments, really," Pest said. "And they're more suggestions than what you'd call actual commandments, but yes."

A nervous grin spread across Drake's face. "Nah!" he said. "You're having a laugh."

"What's so difficult to believe?" Pestilence asked. "I mean, we're the Four Horsemen of the Apocalypse—"

"Three Horsemen," Drake said firmly. "You're the Three Horsemen of the Apocalypse, plus me."

"Well, whatever," said Pestilence, waving a gloved hand. "The point is, we're living proof that it's all true."

"Or you're three lunatics living in a shed in la-la land," Drake said.

"Three lunatics with a flying horse," War said gruffly.

"It didn't fly, it *galloped*," Drake reminded him, although he had to admit the horse going airborne was a difficult one to explain away. "And what about those metal ball things? Don't tell me they were from the Bible too."

War shifted in his seat. "No, they weren't. We're still looking into that one."

"Looking into it? They nearly killed me!"

"Aye, *nearly*. But they didn't, thanks to me. A wee bit of

gratitude wouldn't go amiss."

"*Thank* you?" Drake spluttered.

War nodded. "Don't mention it."

There was a crunching sound to Drake's right. He turned to find Famine cramming popcorn into his mouth with butter-soaked fingers. "Don't mind me," Famine said, spilling a mouthful of half-chewed kernels down his front. "Carry on. It's entertaining, this."

Drake looked away as Famine began scooping the popcorn mush from his stained tracksuit top and licking it from his fingertips.

"Forget the balls for a minute," War said. "Think about the bigger picture. Heaven. Hell. It's all real."

"And not just Heaven and Hell, neither," Pestilence said. "It's all about belief, see?"

"Don't confuse him," War said. "Let him get his head round one thing at a time."

"No, tell me it all," Drake insisted. "I want to know."

Pestilence's eyes darted in War's direction. Eventually, War gave a shrug. "Right, fire on."

"OK, well, you know parallel dimensions?" Pestilence began enthusiastically. "The idea that there are these other realities running alongside this one, sort of the same, but a bit different?"

"Like, alternate universes and stuff?" Drake asked.

"Yes, exactly!" Pestilence clapped. "Well, it's all complete nonsense. There's only this universe."

"Oh," said Drake. "Then why are you telling me?"

"Because there's only this *universe*, but there are many afterlives. There are no parallel Earths, but there *are* parallel afterlives."

"I don't follow."

"There's Heaven and Hell, obviously," Pestilence continued, "you know about them. But there's also Valhalla, afterlife of the Vikings; the Greeks had Hades and the River Styx and all that... Which reminds me, Mount Olympus, where the Greek Gods live – you will love it! Trust me." Pestilence pressed a hand to his chest, as if clutching at his heart. "It's *gorgeous*. Do you like wrestling? If you like wrestling, then—"

"No, I don't like wrestling," Drake interjected. "Can we crack on?"

"Right, sorry," Pestilence said breathlessly. "Well, let's see, there's Yaxche, the cosmic tree of contentment where Mayans believed they would spend all eternity relaxing in the sun.

There's Adlivun, the undersea domain of Sedna, the She-Cannibal."

"*Sedna the She-Cannibal?*"

"Oh yeah, she imprisons the souls of the wicked, apparently," Pestilence shrugged. "We've never met her, but by all accounts she's a right cow." He looked to the others for help. "Who believes in her again?"

"What do you call 'em?" slobbered Famine. "The ice ones."

"Polar bears?" Drake guessed.

"Inuit," War grunted.

"That's the one," Pestilence said. "The Inuit people believe in Sedna, and other people believe in other things," he continued, "and here's the thing: they're all right. All of them. All those things exist, and they exist because enough people believe – or believed – that they exist. It's like they say, 'Faith can make mountains'."

A hazy, half-remembered Sunday School lesson raised its hand at the back of Drake's mind. "I thought it was *move* mountains?"

"Bad translation," War grunted. "You can't move a mountain, I don't care how much faith you've got. Once you stick a mountain down, it's going nowhere." He glanced briefly at Pestilence. "You might as well tell him the rest."

Pestilence gave a cough and cleared his throat again. He smiled self-consciously, and Drake saw a red rash spread up the horseman's neck. It was either embarrassment or psoriasis, Drake couldn't tell which.

"Faith can make... other things too," Pestilence began. "If enough people believe in something, then, sooner or later, it'll turn up."

Drake wasn't following. "Like what?"

"Well," Pestilence said, giving the word two syllables, "you've probably heard of the Tooth Fairy."

Drake blinked. He looked across the faces of the three men, expecting to see them trying to contain their laughter. Instead, their expressions were deadly serious.

"There's not a Tooth Fairy."

"Yes, there is," Pestilence said.

"No, there isn't," Drake insisted. He looked at War. The giant nodded his confirmation. "*Right*," Drake scoffed. "And I suppose there's an Easter Bunny too?"

Pestilence shot Famine an accusatory look. "Well... there *was*."

"What? Not this again," the fat man protested. "He was

made out of chocolate!"

"He was *carrying* chocolate," War said. "There's a big difference."

"Not from where I was standing," Famine mumbled. He rubbed his blubbery stomach and stared wistfully into space, lost in a fond memory.

"Anyway, all these afterlives and mythological kingdoms," Pestilence continued, "they're all separate, but they're all connected. Certain *beings* – of which you are now officially one, *yay!* – can travel between them."

"I don't believe that," Drake said. He crossed his arms across his chest.

"Which bit?" Pestilence asked.

"Any of it. All of it, whatever," Drake told him. He shrugged. "I don't believe any of what you just said."

War's chair scraped across the floor. He stood up, but had to duck his head to avoid bumping it against the roof. "Right, then, in that case we'll just have to prove it." He looked down at Drake. The small patch of face Drake could see behind the big man's beard seemed to darken.

"Tell me," War growled. "What do you know about Limbo?"

CHAPTER TWELVE

THE HARSH WINDS of nothingness whistle around him as he streaks through realms undreamed of by the minds of men. He sees the birth of planets and of suns and of vast, sprawling galaxies, and he pays them no heed.

He is there for the other end of creation too. He alone bears witness to the deaths of other worlds, other stars, other universes. For these he does pause, just briefly, to admire the end of all things.

He crosses each dimension between the beats of his black heart. Each one he travels through brings him closer to his goal. Every realm he passes across, from the ancient to the new, brings him one step nearer to his destiny.

And one step nearer to the shed.

CHAPTER THIRTEEN

I T HAD BEEN nine years since Drake had been to Sunday
School, and even then he'd only gone twice.

The first time he'd gone because he'd heard there was
going to be a puppet show, and Drake liked puppets. He
particularly liked Bert and Ernie, from *Sesame Street*. Or,
at least, he liked Ernie, the fun-loving one with the rubber
duck. He wasn't all that fussed about the po-faced Bert, if he
were completely honest, but even back then he'd instinctively
known the two came as a package.

The Sunday School show didn't feature Bert or Ernie,
though. It didn't even feature a rubber duck. Instead, the
puppet show was about some guy called Jesus healing
something called 'the leper'.

Drake hadn't really known what a leper was, but he'd been

disappointed by the build quality of the puppet. Every time it moved, bits kept falling off. By the time Jesus got round to healing it, it was little more than a torso with a head.

The second time Drake went to Sunday School was to pick up his coat, which he'd forgotten to take home the previous week. It was during this second session, that he had heard about Limbo. And the bit about moving mountains.

Limbo, he had been told, was a place of absolute emptiness, somewhere between Heaven and Hell. It was sort of a neutral territory – a place for souls who hadn't done anything bad enough to earn themselves a ticket to eternal damnation, but who equally hadn't impressed the man upstairs enough to be allowed into Paradise.

At least, that was how Drake remembered the lesson. There was other stuff too, but he'd been busy looking for his jacket by that point, and hadn't really paid all that much attention.

Which was probably just as well, since more or less everything the Sunday School teacher had tried to tell him was wrong.

✦

Drake stood in the doorway of the shed, looking out on to a vast expanse of sand. Overhead, the sky was a wishy-washy sort of blue – nice, but with a chance of scattered showers later.

He turned away from the door and looked to the three men standing behind him. "How did you do that?" he asked, his voice shaking. "Where's my house?"

"The house is where we left it," War assured him. "It's the shed that's moved. We're no longer on Earth. We are in Limbo."

Drake looked out at the copper-coloured sand. Despite everything, he felt surprisingly calm. "It's like... Mars or somewhere."

War and Pestilence stifled a laugh. "'*Mars*'," War smirked. "*Now* who's living in la-la land?"

"I could just go a Mars," Famine panted, salivating slightly. "Don't suppose anyone's got one?"

Drake stepped out on to the sand. It wasn't hot, like he'd expected. In fact, the sand wasn't really anything, temperature-wise. Nor was the air, he noticed. He was neither hot, nor cold, but he didn't feel *just right*, either. It wasn't that he was at the perfect temperature, it was more the case that there was no temperature to speak of.

He looked out across the vast plain. It stretched out as far as the eye could see. Desolate. Bare. Empty.

"Hello, 'ello!"

Drake spun, kicking up a cloud of sand that quickly settled again without a breeze to keep it afloat. A blond-haired man with a goatee beard poked his head round the corner of the shed. He gave Drake a friendly wave.

"Um... hello," Drake said.

The stranger stepped out from behind the shed and looked Drake up and down. At the same time, Drake studied him. The man wore black trousers with a matching black polo neck top and a charcoal-grey waistcoat. His black shoes looked as if they had once been polished, but the sand had taken its toll and now they were scuffed and dull.

The man hooked his thumbs through the belt loops of his trousers and rocked back on his heels. "So," he said, still smiling, "who are you, then?"

Drake glanced sidelong into the shed. Or, at least, he tried to, but the door was now closed.

"Drake," he said. "Drake Finn."

"Alfred Randall," said Alfred Randall, "of the *Alfred*

Randall X-perience." He took one of Drake's hands in both of his and shook it vigorously. He went on like that for several seconds, showing no sign of stopping. Eventually, Drake pulled his hand away.

"So, what you doing in this old thing, then?" asked Alfred, giving the shed a pat. "They in?" He stepped past Drake and tried the door handle. The handle turned, but the door remained firmly closed. "Yoo-hoo! Anyone home? It's Alfred Randall. The *Alfred Randall X-perience.*"

There was silence inside the shed. Alfred turned, his eyes suddenly narrow with suspicion. "Here, you haven't nicked it, have you?"

"No, I haven't nicked it," Drake replied. "They're in there, look." He knocked on the door. "Stop mucking about, there's someone here who wants to talk to you."

At first, Drake heard nothing from beyond the door. Then there was the sound of War muttering below his breath, and the door slowly creaked open. Pestilence emerged first. He wore a floppy white hat and blinked in the sudden glare of the light. War came out next, still muttering. He fired Drake a look of contempt as he stepped on to the sand.

Famine shuffled out next, keeping one hand on the shed wall for support.

"There's the lads!" Alfred cried. He held up a hand for a high-five. When it was clear no one was about to give him one, he clicked his fingers, pointed, then let his hand swing down by his side again. "The lads, the lads, howay the lads!"

"All right, Alf?" War said, with the tone of someone who'd been through this too many times before.

"You can come out, Brian," Alfred shouted. "It's just the lads, right enough!"

"Hello, lads," beamed another man, leaning his head round the corner. The rest of him followed close behind, and Drake realised he was dressed identically to Alfred. He had the same black trousers, shoes and polo shirt, and the same charcoal-coloured waistcoat. He had the same goatee beard too, although his hair was a silvery grey, not blond like Alfred's. He looked older than Alfred, by two decades at least.

"Brian," said Pestilence. He forced a polite smile.

"You're missing one, I see," Alfred said, taking a peek inside the shed and finding it empty. "Where's himself?"

"He's gone," War said, giving nothing away. "This is his replacement."

"Hear that, Brian? This is the new you-know-who!" He shook Drake's hand again. "Pleasure to meet you. Alfred Randall, the *Alfred Randall X-perience*. But then, I expect they've told you all about that?"

Drake glanced over to the Horsemen. They nodded encouragingly.

"Uh... no," Drake said. He heard Pestilence stifle a sob. "Actually, they haven't."

A flicker of pain passed behind Alfred's eyes. His lips pursed together so tightly they virtually disappeared.

"But it's my first day," Drake added quickly.

Alfred smiled. This seemed to satisfy him.

"Well, that explains it," he said. "I'm Alfred Randall, and *we*" – he put an arm round Brian's shoulder and pulled him in – "are the *Alfred Randall X-perience*, Limbo's premier barbershop quartet. And, by the way, that's X as in the letter X," Alfred explained. "*X-perience*." He grinned too broadly. It was the grin, Drake thought, of a man on the edge. "It's not exactly the traditional spelling, but then again, we're not exactly a traditional barbershop quartet, are we, Brian?"

Brian shook his head. "No. There's only the two of us, for a start."

"*And* we do the twiddly bits, don't we, Brian? Show him your twiddly bits."

Brian opened his mouth and made a sound quite unlike anything Drake had heard before. He imagined it was the type of sound a camel might make, were it to attempt to gargle a cat.

Alfred held his hands out at his sides, his point apparently proven. "Let's see the Acapella Afterlifers do *that*, eh?" he said, between snorts of laughter. "Not a friggin' hope!"

"Who are the Acapella—?"

"Right, nice to see you again, Alf, Brian, but we need to get a move on," said War hurriedly. He clamped a hand on Drake's shoulder and pulled him away from the men.

"Ah, always busy, right, lads?" Alfred said. "Any word on the old... you-know-what, yet?" He tapped the side of his nose. "Just between you and I, of course."

"Nothing yet," said War.

"Ah well, keep us posted. Nice to see you again, lads." A thought struck Alf. He turned to Brian, his manic grin advancing further across his face. "Here, Bri, why don't we give the lads a proper *Alfred Randall X-perience* send-off? Sing them on their way, sort of thing?" Alf turned back. "What do you say to that, lads?" he asked.

But the lads were gone.

✦

Drake trudged across the sand, just a few metres behind War. Pestilence followed right behind him. Somewhere in the middle distance, Famine puffed and wheezed in slow pursuit.

"So, I thought Limbo was supposed to be empty?" Drake ventured. "I thought that was the entire point?"

"It was empty, once upon a time," Pestilence told him. "But cram a few million lost souls in and it starts to feel a lot less roomy, if you know what I mean?"

Drake nodded. That made sense, he supposed. "Right. What's with all the *Barbershop X-press* stuff, or whatever they were called?"

"There's not a lot to do in Limbo," Pestilence explained. "So a few thousand years ago they started forming singing groups. No instruments, obviously, just voices. Some of them are really quite good. Some of them... aren't."

"And some of them are the *Alfred Randall X-perience*," added War, with a shudder.

"Quite a few rivalries have developed over the centuries," continued Pestilence. "The *Alfred Randall X-perience* hates the *Acapella Afterlifers*. The *Acapella Afterlifers* can't stand the *Limbo Lyrical All Stars*. And everyone hates the *We Are Voice Experience*."

"Christ," War muttered. "*The WAVE*. I'd forgotten about them." He glanced at the dunes on either side of them, as if anticipating an ambush.

"It's grown into quite a lively old place," Pestilence went on.

Drake looked around. Apart from Famine, who was now almost too far away to see, there was nothing in any direction. Even the shed had long since disappeared beyond the horizon.

"Yeah, it's not *very* lively," Drake began, before his face thudded into War's lower back.

"We've arrived," the giant said.

"About time too," Pestilence complained. "I've got blisters on my blisters, and this sand is doing my dermatitis no favours, let me tell you."

"Sorry, where have we arrived?" Drake asked. He leaned round War, expecting to see more nothing. Instead, he saw a door.

The door was a glossy white with a brass handle situated almost exactly in the centre. There was a wooden frame round the door, painted to match, on to which the door's hinges had been screwed. The door and frame stood upright on the sand, with no walls above or around them.

There was a sign on the door. It was small and rectangular, black in colour, with a gold-painted border. There were two words printed on the sign, also in gold. Drake read them out loud.

"Staff only," he said.

"Right then, sunshine," War said. His powerful hand wrapped round the door knob. "Walk this way and do not – I repeat, do *not* – touch anything."

CHAPTER FOURTEEN

IT WAS DARK on the other side of the door, and the air smelled faintly of damp. War felt along the rough brick wall until he found the light switch. He flicked it on and the darkness was swept away by a sterile white glow.

Row after row of lights came on with a *clunk*. As they did, more and more of the room was revealed.

At first, Drake thought they were in a garage. Then he thought they were in a warehouse. By the time the last row of lights had come on, he could only imagine they were in an aircraft hanger, and a large aircraft hanger, at that.

He was wrong every time. There were no aircraft hangers in Limbo, and no garages, either. There *was* a warehouse, if you knew where to look, but this wasn't it.

"Where did this come from?" Drake asked. He turned

and pressed his hands against the wall. "Bricks," he mumbled. "These are... are... *bricks*. How is that possible? There weren't any bricks a minute ago."

"Oh, don't ask us how it works," Pest said. He took a neatly folded plastic bag from his pocket and opened it. Then he removed his hat, carefully folded it flat, and slipped it into the bag for safekeeping. "Just accept that it does. Trust me, you'll save yourself all kinds of headaches. Nod and smile, that's what I say. Nod and smile."

Drake nodded, but he didn't smile. He turned back, keeping one hand on the wall to make sure it didn't go anywhere, and tried to take in the enormity of the room before him.

He estimated it to be about twenty football pitches long, and the same across. Then again, he had no real idea how big one football pitch was, so this was a wild guess at best.

It was difficult to judge the size of the room with any accuracy, because of its contents. Vast mountains of boxes and bags reached from the floor to somewhere near the ceiling. They stretched out, forming canyons and valleys between the peaks.

There were cardboard boxes, wooden crates, plastic storage tubs and slatted pallets laden with yet more containers. There were black bags, green bags, string bags and hessian sacks, all bulging close to bursting point.

In among it all Drake spotted fourteen rolled-up lengths of carpet, eleven broken picture frames, two vacuum cleaners and a snooker table with a leg missing; all within fifteen metres of where he was standing.

"The Junk Room," Pestilence announced. He saw the wonder etched on Drake's face. "Over the years it's sort of become a storage space for the afterlife. It's where Heaven, Hell and all the others put the stuff they never use, but can't bring themselves to throw away," he explained.

Drake thought about this. There had been a cupboard in his old house, under the stairs. For as long as he could remember it had been full of taped-up boxes, bulging bin bags and a cardboard owl he'd made when he was eight. The entire contents of the cupboard had been packed into the removal van when they'd left the old house, then placed in their entirety in another cupboard in the new house, whereupon the door to that cupboard had been closed.

This, he guessed, was a bit like that, only on a much larger scale.

"Ready for your first challenge?" War asked, turning to face him.

The big man's voice roused Drake from his daze. "Yeah, sorry, what?"

"Your first challenge," War said again. "Are you ready?"

Drake shook his head. "What? 'First challenge'? What do you mean?"

"In order to become the fourth horseman, you must overcome a series of ancient challenges," War explained impatiently.

"Whoa, what? No one told me about ancient challenges."

"Must've slipped my mind," War replied.

"Yeah, that seems to happen a lot," Drake said. "What if I say 'no'?"

"Then you will be cast for ever into the fiery pits of—"

"OK, OK, I get it," Drake sighed. "Fine. What do I have to do?"

War gestured at the landscape of junk strewn ahead of them. "Somewhere within this room is the Robe of Sorrows, a flowing robe woven from darkness itself, which will be worn by the fourth horseman upon the Day of Judgement."

Drake could guess what was coming next. "And you want me to find it."

"And we want... Oh. Aye," said War, looking slightly

deflated. "That's the first challenge. Find the Robe of Sorrows."

"Is that it?" Drake asked. He pointed to a hook on the back of the door. A black robe hung from it, dangling all the way down to the stone floor.

War's eyes went from the robe to Drake, then back again. He quietly cleared his throat. "Right. Well. Aye. The second challenge," he said, moving along quickly. "Hidden in this room is the Deathblade, the long-handled scythe that will be wielded by the fourth horseman upon the Day—"

"All right, all right," Drake muttered. He cast his eyes across the mountainous territory before him. "Any clues?"

"No," said War firmly. He was clearly still annoyed about the cape thing. "No clues."

"But," said Pestilence, pointing towards a distant ridge of box files and ring binders. He gave Drake a wink. "It's probably somewhere over that way."

⊹

Drake clambered up a steep incline, using a string of Christmas tree lights to heave himself along. The boxes he was walking on were cardboard, but packed full enough that they didn't crumple or give way beneath his weight. A few of the boxes tinkled like breaking glass when he stepped on them. He ignored those, and quickly pushed on.

He had been walking, and occasionally scrambling, for fifteen minutes, but had not yet reached the crest of the first hill. He had tried to make his way round the side of the mountain, but the path had been blocked by an outcrop of *Beano* annuals, leaving him no choice but to make for the summit.

When he eventually made it to the top, his heart sank. Twenty football pitches, he realised, was nowhere near big enough.

The room was so large, it had its own horizon. From up there, Drake could see seventeen or eighteen more junk mountains, and too many valleys and glens to count. They were spread out beyond the limits of his vision, and Drake realised that finding the Deathblade might well be an impossible task.

The ridge Pest had pointed him towards was down on his left, near the foot of the mountain. He should go there, he thought. He should definitely go there. And yet, something nagged at the base of his skull. Something made him turn his head and look towards a cliff face half a mile or so away on his right. Something whispered directly into his brain. *Come*, it said, or was he imagining it?

He looked down at the ridge, set his jaw decisively, and went left. A moment later, he changed his mind, about-turned, and set off down the hillside towards the distant cliff.

✛

Drake stood at the bottom of the cliff face, looking up. It had looked high from the mountaintop. Down here, ankle-deep in old knitting patterns and gardening magazines, it looked infinitely higher.

It was made up mostly of plastic storage boxes, the type designed to be stacked, one on top of the other. Clearly someone had begun stacking, and then forgotten to stop.

The feeling that had drawn Drake to that spot now drew him upwards. The bottom of each box was slightly narrower than the top, creating a ladder-like series of handholds all the way up the side of the cliff.

Still, it was a long way to the top. He thought about looking for another route up, but the whispering in his brain was louder now, and he wasn't sure he could resist it, even if he wanted to.

Climb, the voice hissed as he reached up and found the first handhold. *Climb!*

✧

Drake pulled himself up another few storage tubs. His arms should have been aching. His shoulders should have burned with the effort. But they didn't. He wasn't tired and he wasn't sore.

He *was* terrified, though, having made the mistake of looking down a few minutes after he'd started to climb. Even then, the ground had looked to be a dizzyingly long way away. He'd been moving steadily upwards for ten minutes or more since then, and had no plans to look down again.

Had he thought about it, Drake would've realised it all felt too easy, as if someone else had taken control of his limbs. His fingers did not slip. His feet did not falter. He scaled the vertical face with ease.

At the top of the cliff was another cliff. It was set five or six metres back from the edge of the first one, and stretched almost as high as it had. Drake did not realise how high this second cliff was, though, because he didn't look up.

Instead, he looked into the dark, rectangular hole situated

almost directly in front of him. It was about five metres high by three wide, and seemed to lead directly into the storage-box mountain.

Cautiously, Drake approached the opening. A cool breeze tickled his skin, sending goosebumps along the length of his arm. It was the first time he had felt the air move since entering Limbo and, although he couldn't explain why, it made him nervous.

"Hello?" he called into the void. "Anyone there?"

A voice called to him. Was it still in his head, or had he heard it out loud this time? He couldn't say, but it didn't matter. The words had meant the same thing.

I am the Deathblade, it said. *Come to me.*

Unbidden, Drake's legs began to move. His feet made a series of hollow *thuds* on the lids of the plastic tubs below him as he strode into the cave and was swallowed by the darkness within.

CHAPTER FIFTEEN

I N A YAWNING CHASM between one world and another, he stops. There is a moment when he feels... *something*. A sensation. An emotion. Newly born, he cannot yet put a name to the feeling, but in time he will come to know it as "confusion".

He is confused because it has moved. The shed has moved.

His ghastly outline turns. His gaze sweeps back across the realms he has already traversed. The worlds blur around him as he sets off again in the opposite direction, moving faster than he has ever moved before.

CHAPTER SIXTEEN

D RAKE FUMBLED THROUGH the dark, feeling his way along a plastic wall, deeper into the heart of the mountain. The cool breeze blew past him, making him shiver just slightly. From up ahead he could hear a low drone, but the blackness within the cave made it impossible to see what was causing the sound.

He stopped, and knelt down on the hard plastic floor. His fingers found the edge of a box lid and undid the flimsy clasps. He felt inside the open container, hoping to find a torch or lantern or something. But the box contained what felt like photographs and postcards, and a small wooden wind chime.

He closed the lid and moved on to the next box. There was a tangle of cables inside; an impossible knot of wires and extension cords. Not what he was looking for.

The next box was filled with wooden cups, shaped like old-fashioned goblets. The next had two flat rectangles of stone, one atop the other. There was writing carved into the surface of the top stone, but Drake couldn't tell what it said.

Another box contained CDs, mostly, and a few books. The next one appeared to be filled with salt. Something *hissed* and *snarled* in the box after that one. Drake decided not to open it, and moved on to the next.

He decided to check two more of the plastic containers. If he didn't find anything to light the way by then, he would turn back. There was no way he was carrying on in the dark, regardless of what the whispering voice in his head might say.

Drake didn't know what was in the next box, but the smell was enough to make him close the lid without checking too closely. It smelled a lot like Toxie the Hellcat, but with a burned-meat edge to it that made Drake's eyes stream.

He crawled over to the next box and put his hands on the lid.

Then he took them off again. A feeling, like the one that had led him to the cave, steered him three boxes to the left.

His fingers found the lid's plastic clasps and a feeling of warmth spread along both arms.

Drake opened the lid and the sound of a choir rang out from within the tub. A bright, brilliant light flooded the cave. Drake screwed his eyes shut and covered them with both arms, but the light still shone through. Blinded, Drake reached clumsily into the box. His fingers wrapped round some kind of hoop and he pulled it free.

He clicked the lid back into place and the music stopped. The blinding light went with it, leaving only the glow of the object in Drake's hand to chase away the darkness in the cave.

Drake looked at the thing he was holding. It was a ring of glowing white light, about the size of a dinner plate. The light itself was solid enough for Drake to hold.

It felt warm to the touch, and the surface of the light seemed to move beneath his grip. It was a bit like holding on to a pipe, through which warm water was running, but a magical glowing pipe, that made you want to shout "Hallelujah!" as loudly and as often as you could. Even with everything he'd seen recently, this seemed particularly incredible.

Drake lowered the ring towards the floor. The shadows fled from its warm glow, revealing a printed label stuck to the lid of the plastic box.

HALOS, the label read. (ASSORTED SIZES)

Now come, the voice in his head insisted. Drake did as he was told. Holding the halo out before him to light the way, he continued down the plastic passageway towards whatever lay ahead.

The cave came to a stop twenty or so metres later, in a wall of brightly coloured stackable tubs. A slim wooden wardrobe stood against the wall, its double doors tied together with string. The air was colder around the wardrobe, and Drake found himself rubbing his arms to try to keep warm.

His breath clouded into mist as he opened his mouth and said, "Hello?"

No reply came. Drake took a step closer to the wardrobe. It looked like a cheap, flat-packed one, which surprised him. If the Deathblade was as powerful a weapon as War had said, why keep it in a flimsy wardrobe? In fact, why keep it in a wardrobe at all?

"Hello?" he said again, raising his voice to be heard above the low droning noise that filled this part of the cave. The voice in his head stayed silent.

Drake raised the halo, casting its eerie yellow light across the walls and the ceiling. Above the wardrobe were four large vents. The cold breeze was blowing from within them. An air-conditioning system in a land without temperature. But why?

Welcome, chimed the whispers in his brain. *I am the Deathblade. Have you come to claim my power?*

"Uh... yeah," Drake said. "I think so."

Then come. Claim the power of the Deathblade as your own.

"Where are you?"

There was a pause. *Guess.*

"Are you... are you in the wardrobe?" Drake asked.

I am in the wardrobe, the voice confirmed.

Drake took another step. "The handles are tied together," he said.

Oh. Right, said the Deathblade. *Who's done that, then?*

"Dunno."

Someone playing silly beggars, I expect.

"Yeah, probably," Drake said. He felt like he was losing his already slim grip on the situation. "Want me to untie it?"

Go on, then.

Drake approached the wardrobe. The draught from the air-conditioning was freezing. His fingers were beginning to feel numb as he hooked the halo over his wrist, and reached for the knots in the string.

Oh, but before you do, the voice said, *those who seek to claim the Deathblade's power, must first face the Deathblade Guardian.*

Drake stopped untying the string. He looked the wardrobe up and down, as if its expression might somehow give something away.

"Deathblade Guardian?" he asked. "What's that?"

POP.

A few metres away on Drake's right, the lid of one of the plastic boxes that made up the floor sprang open. It landed with a *clatter* somewhere close to Drake's feet.

In the glow of the halo, Drake saw an arm pull itself free of the box. The arm was around fifty centimetres long from the tip of the fingers to the elbow, where it ended in a tangle of wires. It was metal, chrome in colour, and had pyramid-shaped spikes jutting up from every knuckle where the fingers met the hand.

Drake watched the robotic arm drag itself slowly towards

him. He didn't move back. As arms went, it was a nasty-looking one, but it was, after all, just an arm.

POP.

Another lid flew into the air behind him. Another arm, identical to the first, dragged itself out. Drake turned side-on so he could see both of them. They crawled closer, pulling themselves across the floor on their long metal fingers.

"OK..." Drake muttered, suddenly feeling much less confident.

POP, went another lid. *POP. POP. POP.*

Drake spun. Robotic body parts were emerging from the floor all around him, like the final act of a future-set zombie movie. Sections of upper arm and of metallic thigh wriggled like snakes across the box lids. Two armoured feet hopped towards him, their metal shins pointing towards the cave ceiling.

Drake felt the cold touch of metal against his ankle. He leaped sideways and let out a little shriek. The hand clattered back down on to the hollow floor and Drake darted a few metres to the left, keeping out of its reach.

The body parts did not move to follow him. They kept hopping and squirming and crawling towards the spot where he'd been standing. With a *whirr* and a *clank*, the forearms connected with the upper arms, and the shins joined with the metal thighs.

"What the Hell is this?" Drake muttered, as the arms reached into other boxes and pulled out more parts. A chestplate. Two round shoulders, studded with deadly-looking spikes.

There was more whirring, more clanking, as these parts and more attached themselves to one another. Drake watched, awestruck and terrified in equal measures as the limbs connected with the newly formed torso.

POP!

A final box opened. Two long, curved horns rose up, followed by a gleaming metal skull. The skull's mouth was fixed in a malevolent grin that stretched almost all the way up to its hollow eye-sockets.

The skull clambered out of the box, carried on eight spindly metal legs that extended from within its neck. It scurried like a spider across the floor, before rolling into position next to the chest.

The metal legs gripped the top of the chestplate and pulled the skull into position. Wires squirmed from the neck and from the body, joining together, forming connections.

With a *clunk*, the skull snapped into place. Deep in its eye-sockets, a dull red light began to glow. Metal squeaked, and the robot sat upright. The horned head swivelled 180 degrees until it was looking directly at Drake.

Behold the Deathblade Guardian, said the voice in Drake's head. *Defeat it and claim the power of the Deathblade, or else die in the attempt.*

The Deathblade Guardian raised itself up on its hydraulic legs and looked down at Drake. Drake looked up at the Deathblade Guardian.

"Um, hi," he said.

And then he ran away.

CHAPTER SEVENTEEN

THE VOICE IN Drake's head screamed angrily at him, ordering him to turn back. Drake ignored it and powered on along the passageway, racing towards the exit. Behind him, he heard the hollow *thunk, thunk, thunk* of heavy footsteps hitting the plastic floor. He glanced back over his shoulder, but the light from the halo only reached a few metres, and all he could see of the Deathblade Guardian were its two red eyes burning in the dark.

A robotic demon. War hadn't mentioned any snap-together robotic demons guarding the scythe. Something else that had 'slipped his memory', no doubt.

Something whistled past Drake's ear. He chanced another look back. The light from the entrance up ahead lifted away the veil of shadow. The polished chrome of the guardian came stomping from the darkness, one clenched fist raised.

There was a puff of smoke, a flash of flame, and a pyramid-shaped knuckle rocketed towards Drake's head. Drake ducked and stumbled, and the missile streaked harmlessly past. It hit the side of a plastic tub at a shallow angle, and ricocheted into the softening gloom up ahead.

The Deathblade Guardian marched on, the plastic floor buckling beneath its immense weight as it closed the gap between it and Drake. Its arm remained raised, the fist trained on the boy's back. Another flash. Another puff of smoke. Drake barely had time to twist sideways. He felt the turbulence the spike caused as it streaked by him.

"Look, keep the scythe," Drake cried. "I don't want it."

The clanking and thudding of the robot seemed to be right behind him. He daren't look back now. Had to keep moving, keep running, get to the exit and get away.

The lights of the Junk Room weren't particularly bright, but they dazzled him as he stumbled from inside the cave. He took a brief moment to get his bearings, and then a somewhat more leisurely moment to realise he was trapped.

One cliff face led upwards, the other led down to the ground far below. He had climbed quickly, but there was no way he would be fast enough to make it up or down before the guardian could take aim.

A whirring of hydraulics behind him made Drake spin round. The demonic figure of the robot *clanked* out from the confines of the cave. Its polished metal frame glinted in the glow from the overhead lights. Its demented grin seemed to twist further up its unmoving face, as the twin red circles in its eye-sockets glowed even brighter.

Drake backed towards the edge of the cliff. A weapon, he needed a weapon. If only he had some sort of—

His eyes went to the halo in his hand. It looked like the flying disc he'd been given for his birthday a couple of years ago. It had been a fun gift. Perhaps not as much fun as the games console he'd asked for, but he'd become pretty good with it in the weeks after his birthday.

The guardian's clenched fist briefly tightened. The final projectile on its left hand streaked across the gap between the boy and the robot. Drake dropped to one knee, curled the halo in against his chest, then flicked out sharply with his wrist.

The hoop of holy light spun as it sliced through the air towards the Deathblade Guardian. Drake followed its flight, praying to whichever deity was listening that his aim was good.

It was. The spinning ring found its target. "Yes, yes, *yes*!" Drake cheered as the halo struck the guardian across its exposed metal throat.

"No, no, *no*," he groaned, when the glowing hoop bounced harmlessly off the robot, and clattered noisily to the ground.

The mechanical demon clanked closer, its arm still raised, fist still clenched. But, Drake realised, the knuckle-spikes were all used up. He may not have a weapon, but nor did the Deathblade Guardian!

There was a sound in Drake's head, like a snigger. The robot lowered its left arm...

...and then raised its right one. Four more pyramid-shaped projectiles took aim at Drake's head. The robot was too close now, and Drake was too near the cliff edge. There was no way he could dodge another attack.

He saw the guardian clench its fist tighter. Drake's hands went to the lid of the box by his feet. The clasps unclipped as four puffs of smoke and four fiery flashes sent four little missiles hurtling towards him.

The lid wouldn't stop a direct hit, he knew, but if he could angle it correctly, like the wall back in the cave, he might stand a chance. He thrust the rectangle of plastic out in front of his face, tilted upwards.

A sound like machine-gun fire rattled across the lid's surface. The force of four impacts almost sent him toppling backwards over the edge of the cliff, but he held his ground and laughed, half with relief, half with amazement, when the spikes deflected upwards to be lost in the vastness of the Junk Room.

He didn't laugh for long. A pincer grip tore the lid from his hands. Drake found himself looking up into the red-eyed glare of the guardian.

"Can't we talk about this?" he pleaded.

A metal arm reared back, a metal fist was driven down towards him. Drake rolled clumsily and the fist punched a hole through another plastic lid. The hand raised again, bringing the entire storage box with it.

The guardian shook its arm, flicking its hand up and down as it attempted to dislodge the box. Seizing the opportunity, Drake leaped to his feet and drove a shoulder against the robot's back, trying to knock it off balance.

Something buzzed across his skin and through his bones as he made contact with the Deathblade Guardian. A shock of energy pushed him away, and sent him spiralling down on to the floor. He skidded on the smooth plastic and slid, screaming, towards the sheer drop.

His hands grabbed at the edge of a box lid as he slipped across it. His fingers, curved into claws, caught hold just as his legs swung out over the cliff edge. Bicycling wildly with both feet, he dragged himself back on to slightly more solid ground and rolled over on to his back.

The metal demon turned its attention away from the box on its arm. It took two clanking steps towards Drake and raised a knee to the level of its chest.

A foot came down. Drake squirmed into the shape of a letter C, and a metal heel was driven straight through the lid of another box, right where Drake's stomach had been a half-second before.

Drake scrambled out of the guardian's reach. The robot wobbled unsteadily, its right foot deep inside a storage tub, its left foot still standing atop the next box over. It was right at the edge of the cliff. Drake knew he wouldn't get another chance like it.

He scurried, crab-like on his hands and feet over to where the robot teetered, and stopped at the box the metal foot was stuck in. The horned skull turned to face him. The red eyes burned with mechanical fury. Drake dug his heels against the edge of the box's lid, gritted his teeth, and pushed.

The guardian's own size worked against it. As soon as the box began to move, the robot's weight helped to increase its momentum. The one hand of the Deathblade Guardian that wasn't stuck inside a plastic box reached out and grabbed for Drake, but it was too late. As the top box fell away from the cliff, it brought the others below it along for the ride.

The robot let out a high-pitched whine, as the vertical stack of a hundred or more plastic storage boxes toppled like a felled tree towards the ground far, far below.

Drake watched the tumbling demon-shaped figure until it smashed hard against the junk-strewn floor. He kept watching for another few minutes, but it didn't get back up.

"I did it," he muttered to himself, scarcely able to believe it. Then, to the voice of the Deathblade, "I did it!"

But the voice of the Deathblade didn't answer.

He had just started walking back towards the cave, when he heard a movement from the far edge of the cliff, where it curved round out of sight. Drake tensed, fearing another attack. He had lucked out against the first guardian, and doubted he'd survive a clash with another one.

A towering figure stepped out from the cliff side. Behind, and slightly below him, a much smaller figure wheezed his way up a flight of steps.

"Never again," panted Pestilence. He took two short puffs on an inhaler and massaged the centre of his chest. "Never... again."

"What you doing up here?" War demanded gruffly. He held Drake in a tractor-beam stare as he strode across the plastic floor. "You were told – the Deathblade is over by that ridge."

"What? No, it isn't," Drake said. He pointed into the cave. "It's in there."

Pestilence mopped some non-existent sweat from his brow with a spotted handkerchief, then placed the handkerchief in a small plastic bag marked: FOR INCINERATION.

"Whatever makes you say that?" he asked.

"Because I heard it," Drake explained. "It called to me."

Pestilence turned to look at War, but War didn't look back, leaving the other Horseman to stare at the back of the giant's head. "That's why you changed direction, is it?" War asked. "We were watching you."

"Yeah," Drake said. "And thanks for telling me about the Deathblade Guardian, by the way. I mean, it wasn't a big problem," he said coolly. "I was able to beat it and everything, but it would've been nice to know about it beforehand."

"Right, aye, sorry," War said. He scratched his chin through his beard. "So, just to recap: you heard the Deathblade calling to you and leading you here, and you managed to defeat its guardian?"

Without really meaning to, Drake puffed out his chest. "That's right."

"You hear that, Pest? The scythe spoke to him, and he leathered seven shades out of the Deathblade Guardian. Amazing that, eh?"

"It is," Pestilence agreed. "It's, um, it's certainly amazing."

Drake shrugged, but couldn't hide his grin. "Yeah, I suppose it was pretty impressive."

"Oh, no, that's not what I meant," War explained. "I didn't mean *you* were amazing. What's amazing is that the scythe cannae talk. It's just a scythe." He took another step closer until his shadow seemed to block out the glow of the overhead lights. "*And*," War continued, "there *is* no Deathblade Guardian."

The words trundled around inside Drake's head, not quite making any sense. "Yes, there is," he said at last. "And yes, it can. It spoke to me. It said someone had been playing silly beggars with its wardrobe."

To his credit, War's face remained completely impassive. "Its wardrobe?"

"Look, I'll show you, it's in here," Drake insisted. He made for the entrance to the cave. "It's just along—"

The mountain beneath their feet trembled as an explosion tore through the cave. Drake and Pestilence hurled themselves to the floor. Only War remained standing as the fire spat, and choking clouds of melting plastic began to spew from the hole in the cliff wall.

Drake raised his head and coughed as the fumes swirled round him. He looked into the cave and saw the darkness licked away by a flickering wall of flame.

"The Deathblade!" he yelped.

"It isn't there," War told him. "It was never there. It's

down by the ridge, where Pest hid it yesterday."

Drake looked up at War, then back into the burning cave. Gloopy strands of melting plastic dangled like stalactites from the ceiling. Or was it *stalagmites*? He could never remember.

"So... if it wasn't the scythe calling me," he began, voicing the question that was bothering all three of them, "what was it?"

"I don't know," War admitted gravely. "But I suggest we don't hang around to find out. All in favour?"

"Seconded," said Pestilence, raising a rubber-gloved hand from his position, face-down on the floor.

"Sounds good to me," Drake agreed. "But it's a steep climb."

"We took the stairs up," War said. He hoisted both Drake and Pest on to their feet, one in each hand. "It's a pretty safe bet they go all the way back down too."

"I didn't know there were stairs."

"Did you look?"

Drake was about to shoot War a sarcastic response, when he heard the *thunk, thunk, thunk* of plodding, heavy footsteps approaching. He didn't bother to tense up this time, and waited instead for the gargantuan shape to heave itself up the final few steps.

Famine's face was a bright scarlet red when he finally dragged his blubbery frame on to the clifftop. He doubled over after the last step, his slab-like hands resting on his staggeringly bulky knees as he gulped in lungful after lungful of smoky air.

Finally, with several low grunts and groans, Famine straightened himself up. He looked at the others and did his best to fold his gummy lips into a smile. "All right?" he puffed. "What'd I miss?"

CHAPTER EIGHTEEN

D RAKE OPENED THE shed door and looked out. He saw his garden, beyond which lay his house, and, beyond that, his world.

The journey back across the desert of Limbo had been uneventful enough. Before they left the Junk Room, War had collected the Deathblade, which was tightly wrapped in a sheet of blue plastic, and Pestilence had reluctantly agreed to carry the Robe of Sorrows.

Drake had offered to carry both, but had been told by War in no uncertain terms that he was 'nowhere near ready'. And so he had followed behind the two horsemen, doing his best to encourage the waddling Famine along.

From somewhere off in the distance, an a cappella version of *House of the Rising Sun* – without the twiddly bits – had floated tunelessly across the sand. This had made them all pick up their pace, and in no time they were back at the shed. Just a few seconds after that, they were back in Drake's garden.

"So, the second challenge," Drake said, still looking out at the high grass of the garden. "I failed it, didn't I?"

"Yes," War said.

You could've heard a pin drop in the shed.

"What happens now?" Drake asked.

War took almost a full thirty seconds to reply. When he did he sounded hesitant, as if he were unsure of what he was saying. "We'll call it 'outside interference'," he said.

Drake turned to face him. War was back in his usual seat at the table, his face serious, his fingers steepled in front of him. Pestilence was quietly setting up the board game, *Guess Who?* while Famine, for his part, was eating a Twix.

"So what does that mean?" Drake asked.

"The challenge is void. You get an automatic pass."

"Oh, right." Drake thought about this. "Good."

"Yay!" said Pest, shuffling a deck of very small cards with the flair of a Vegas dealer.

Something had been bothering Drake all the way back from the Junk Room. He decided to voice it. "The Deathblade

145

Guardian. Or... whatever it was. It was a robot," he said. "Like those ball things at the school. They were... What did you call it again? Techno-mystical...?"

"Techno-magic mumbo jumbo," said War quietly.

"That's it. Techno-magic mumbo jumbo. Do you think the same person made both of them?"

"Oh, yes," Pest said. He cut the deck, then expertly furrowed the cards back together. "It'll be the old Death. He was right into all his techno-magic mumbo jumbo. I expect he's trying to kill you."

Drake was taken aback by the matter-of-fact tone of that last statement. "Why would he be trying to kill me?"

Pest shrugged. "Jealousy, I'd imagine."

"But he quit! It wasn't my fault!"

Famine shook his head. The movement made his whole upper body wobble like half-set jelly. "No, he went mental, remember? Flipped his lid. No saying what he's capable of now."

Drake blinked. "Oh, well, thanks for that. That's really reassured me, that has."

"Don't worry about it," War said. "Sit down, we can talk about it while we play."

Drake hesitated, then lowered himself on to the seat

across from War. They both had a *Guess Who?* board in front of them.

"We'll do it in rounds," Pest explained. "The winner of you two plays the winner of me and Famine." He fanned the cards and held them out. Drake took one and propped it up in a slot on the board.

For the first time, he looked properly at the little cartoon faces lined up before him. He'd played this game before, but it hadn't looked like this. He read the characters' names aloud.

"Abraham, Jacob, Joseph... What's all this?"

"It's the Bible version," War explained, as he took a card from Pest. He looked at it impassively, then placed it on his board. "I'll start."

"New boy should go first," Famine said. "Only fair."

"That's true," Pest agreed.

"Oh, all right," War scowled. "Get on with it, then."

Drake looked down at the board. He blew out his cheeks. The problem was, most of them looked pretty similar. Near identical, in fact. He decided to take a wild stab. "Do they have a beard?"

War clicked his tongue against his front teeth and leaned

back in his chair. "No," he said quietly.

Drake looked at his board. Then he flipped down every face but one. "Is it the Virgin Mary?"

"Yes," War sighed. He held the card up for the others to see, then threw it down on the table. "Stupid bloody game, anyway."

"Well done, Drake," Pest beamed, as he took back the cards and set the boards up for himself and Famine to play.

"So..." began Drake, looking across at War.

"So what?"

"The old Death. You said we'd talk about him."

War crossed his arms over his chest. "What do you want to know?"

"Well, if he's trying to kill me, I want to know everything," Drake replied.

"He was here for a thousand years. Everything might take a while."

"Well, I never liked him, I don't mind telling you," Pest offered. He was staring intently at his board. "Right, then," he said, eyeballing Famine. "Did he lead the children of Israel out of Egypt?"

Famine shook his head. "Nope."

Pest flipped down the cartoon Moses. "Your turn."

"Why didn't you like him?" Drake asked.

"He just never really fitted in," Pest shrugged. "You'd never catch him doing this, for example."

"Did he beget Isaac?" Famine asked.

"It's not Abraham, no," Pest said. He turned to Drake. "He was more into tinkering with his gadgets. Little robotic creations and what not, like them metal balls and the guardian thing. It was like he preferred their company to ours."

"Really?" asked Drake, trying not to sound sarcastic.

"He was obsessed with the Apocalypse too," Famine added.

Drake frowned. "Aren't you all, though? I mean, isn't that the whole point of you being here?"

"Oh, I mean we're all *interested* in the Apocalypse," Famine said. "We're all *interested* in it, yeah, but he was over the top, he was."

"Was he beheaded?" Pest asked.

Famine blinked. "What, Death?"

"No, the person on your card."

Famine looked down at the board, as if suddenly remembering it was there. "Oh. No," he said. There were a couple of *clacks* as Pest flipped down two more faces.

"I don't understand. In what way was he obsessed?" Drake asked.

"He just banged on about it a lot," War said. "Always wondering what it was going to be like, always complaining that it was taking too long. He just wanted it to hurry up."

"And the longer he waited, the worse he got," Pest added. "On and on he went. On and on."

"Don't you all want it to hurry up, though?" Drake asked.

For a fraction of a second, War said nothing. "Well, aye," he nodded. "Course we do, but the difference is, we don't keep harping on about it."

"Did he beget Achaz?" asked Famine.

"Don't just ask if they begot someone," Pest said. "That makes it boring. Think of other questions."

"All right, all right," Famine grumbled. He looked long and hard at the board in front of him. In the silence of the shed, Drake could almost hear the horseman's brain working.

"Right," Famine said, at last. "Was he the father of Achaz?"

Pest sighed. "No."

Famine nodded. "Right." His eyes went across the faces on his board. "Who was the father of Achaz again?"

"So, that's why he left?" Drake asked, ignoring the ensuing bickering between Pestilence and Famine. "He didn't want to wait any more."

"That's about the size of it," War said. "He said he was going off to make it happen. Said it was his responsibility to make sure it happened."

"And what did you say?"

"'Good riddance, ya nutter.'"

Pest and Famine were still arguing. Drake raised his voice to be heard over them. "And what do you think? Can he actually do it?"

War took a moment to consider this. "He's human now, so probably not."

Drake hadn't realised until that moment that he had been tense, but now he felt himself relax a little. "Right," he said. "That's good to know."

"Although," War said, "if he put things in place before he left, if he had a plan – and God knows, he had enough time to come up with one – then... aye. Maybe he could."

The relief that had washed over Drake drained slowly away. "He could really end the world?"

War nodded gravely. "I wouldn't put it past him."

"And what if he tries to kill me again? What if he sends more robot things?"

"We'll keep our eyes open," War said, but the way he shrugged didn't do much to put Drake at ease.

"Right, I give up," Pest announced in a voice filled with shrill annoyance. "I had Saint James the Lesser, OK? Happy now?" He held up a picture of a bearded man, then stuffed it back into the pack. "Drake, you're playing *him*," he said, glaring at Famine. "Good luck, it's like beating your head against a brick wall."

Drake stood up. "No, I can't hang about," he said. "I need to get home."

War frowned. Pestilence stopped shuffling. Famine took a bite from a Victoria Sponge.

"Home?" War said.

"Yeah, I don't want to be too late – my mum will get worried," Drake told them.

Pest cleared his throat, but didn't say anything. War's leather armour *creaked* as he leaned back in his chair.

"You *are* home, boy," he said. "Your old life – you have to leave that behind. You are no longer Drake Finn, you are the Fourth Horseman. You are the rider on the pale horse. You are Death."

"For the next ninety days," Drake reminded him. "After that, I quit, remember? So, in the meantime, I'm going home, OK?"

None of the horsemen moved to stop him, so Drake left the shed and pulled the door firmly closed behind him.

A few seconds later, the door opened again. "I'll see you tomorrow after school," he said, then he clicked the door closed for a second time, and slipped off into the high grass.

✦

Next morning, Drake walked down the front path, swallowing the last bite of his breakfast. He swung the gate open and strode out, then almost tripped over someone sitting on the pavement.

"Hi. Didn't expect to see you here," said Mel. Her back was leaning against the fence, her legs straight out in front of her, feet together.

Drake's mind raced. His mouth dropped open.

"Now you're supposed to say, 'What, exiting my front garden just before school time?'," Mel prompted.

The vaguely awkward school-gates conversation from yesterday replayed in his head. "Yeah," he mumbled. "What are the chances?"

Mel popped to her feet and brushed some little stones and muck from the back of her skirt. "Mind if I walk you to school?" she asked. "You can say no if you want, but I'll just follow you anyway, shouting abuse." She put a hand to the side of her mouth. "*ABUSE!*" she cried. "See, like that?"

"OK, yeah, that'd be great," Drake said. He began walking, and Mel followed along. "How do you know where I live?" he asked.

Mel shrugged. "I have my sources. But the reason I came – I remembered what I was meant to tell you yesterday."

"Oh, right," said Drake. "What was it?"

"Dr Black."

"Dr Black?"

"Dr Black," Mel repeated. "He came to Mr Franks's class yesterday after you'd left, pretending to be all worried about you."

"How do you know he was pretending?" Drake asked.

"Because he doesn't worry about anyone," Mel said. "So, straight away my suspicions are aroused, I'm like, 'Dr Black, worried about someone? No chance.'"

"Right," said Drake, a little uncertainly. "Was that it?"

"You think I'd walk all the way over here just to tell you that?" Mel scoffed.

"What, then?"

"He started accusing you of stuff. Well, not exactly accusing, but pointing the finger of suspicion, let's say." She prodded him in the chest. "At you."

"What did he say?"

"That you were the last one to see the missing kids."

A frown creased Drake's forehead. "Well, he's lying, I don't even know who they are."

"He said something about... outside the toilets?"

Drake felt his stomach tighten. He stopped walking. "Wait, they're not those three little spotty guys, are they?"

"Yeah, that's them. So... what? You *were* the last to see them?"

"Yeah," said Drake absent-mindedly. "I mean, no, no, I wasn't. He was. He took them away after that. I saw him taking them through a door in his classroom."

"So then he was lying," Mel realised. "Why would he be lying?"

"I don't know," Drake said. He thought about the floating sphere, and about the fact it had come from within the history teacher's classroom. "But I think we'd better try to find out."

CHAPTER NINETEEN

H<small>E CASTS HIS</small> wretched gaze across the sands that stretch into infinity on all sides of him. The whirlpools of his eyes tilt down, down, before finally coming to rest on a rectangular indent on the desert floor. Somewhere, far off to his left, a purely vocal arrangement of Queen's *Another One Bites the Dust* drifts across the plains.

He turns, once more, and slips through the barrier between that dimension and the next.

Again.

CHAPTER TWENTY

WHEN THE BELL rang for morning break, they both knew what they had to do.

Drake had practised the route in his head all morning so he wouldn't waste time finding his way. Even so, Mel made it to Dr Black's room before he did. She was standing by the door, keeping guard, when Drake finally came clattering along the corridor.

"He's out on patrol," Mel told him. "He does it every break and lunchtime, just strides around scowling at everyone. We've got fifteen minutes."

"That should be enough," Drake said. He grasped the door handle, then paused, feeling his heart pick up the pace. The last time he had opened this door he had almost been killed. But Mel was already nudging him, and his hand was already turning the handle.

The door creaked open, revealing a room devoid of any mechanical monsters. Drake let out a shaky breath as Mel brushed past him into the classroom.

"So, what are we looking for, exactly?" she asked, as she slid open a drawer on the teacher's desk.

Drake didn't quite know what to say to that. There had been no need to explain anything to Mel when he asked her to help him sneak into Dr Black's room. She had agreed without asking any questions, and had seemed genuinely excited by the idea. Now, though, even she was starting to look a little apprehensive.

"I don't know," Drake admitted. "But three dead bodies, maybe."

Mel stopped. She slid the drawer closed. "Doubt they'll be in there, then."

"That's the door they went in," Drake said. Mel followed his gaze.

"That's just a cupboard," she said. "Why would he put them in a cupboard?"

"Not for anything good," Drake guessed.

Mel crept past him until she reached the cupboard door.

She looked round the edges, where the door met the frame, as if checking for booby traps. Finally, she placed her hand on the handle.

"Ready?" she asked.

Drake swallowed. He felt more nervous at that moment than he had in the cave back in Limbo. "Ready."

"Here goes," Mel said. She held her breath as she pushed down the handle. The door didn't open. "Well, that's disappointing," she sighed, letting the breath out. She crouched down and studied the keyhole directly below the handle, then put one eye to it. There was only darkness on the other side. "What do we do now?"

Drake joined her at the door. He pressed his ear to the wood, and rapped on it three times. "Hello?" he said.

"Hello," came a reply, but it hadn't come from inside the cupboard. "Can I help you, *children*?" asked Dr Black. He spat the last word out, as if it left a sour taste in his mouth.

"Hi, Dr Black," said Mel, smiling innocently. Her lips were moving before Drake's brain had even realised the need for an excuse. "Drake and I were having an argument about the Second World War. I say D-Day came before V-Day, but he says V-Day came first. I know, he's an idiot, right?

Anyway, we thought, who better to help settle—"

"Silence," Dr Black said.

"To help settle the argument than Dr Black, the most informed history teacher in the whole—"

Dr Black's voice made the windows rattle in their frames. "I said *be quiet*!"

Mel stopped talking. The teacher glared at her for several seconds, the air whistling in and out of his hooked nose as he breathed. When he was certain she wasn't about to start babbling again, he turned his gaze on the boy beside her.

"What are you doing in my room?" he asked. His voice was low and controlled, but menacing enough that anyone hearing it would be in no doubt that it could become very loud again, very quickly.

"We were just looking around," Drake said. From the corner of his eye, he saw Mel wince. But he wasn't trying to make excuses. He wanted the truth. Drake drew himself up to his full height. "We were looking for the kids who went missing. I saw them go into your cupboard."

Dr Black's expression did not change. "Did you, indeed?"

"And you were there," Drake continued. "I saw you," he said, although he realised that this wasn't strictly true.

"And so you suspect I had something to do with their disappearance," Dr Black said. He clicked his tongue against the roof of his mouth. "And who else have you spoken to about this?"

"No one," Drake said. A nagging doubt told him this was the wrong thing to say. The feeling was confirmed when a relieved smile spread across Dr Black's face.

"Lucky for me, then. I dread to think what such wild accusations could do to my reputation, were they to spread to the populace at large."

He looked from Drake to Mel and back again, as if deciding what to do with them. At last, he turned and strode across to the window. "With me, Mr Finn."

Drake hesitated. The classroom door was open. They could make a break for it while the teacher's back was turned. But then what? They'd know nothing more than they knew already, and then they'd always be running from Dr Black.

He walked over to the window, with Mel following along behind him.

"What do you see out there, Mr Finn?" Dr Black asked.

Drake looked through the grubby glass. The classroom was one storey up, giving it a reasonably good view of the rectangle of concrete that made up the bulk of the school grounds.

"Kids," Drake said, looking down at the heads of the children roaming below. "Just kids."

"Look closer." Dr Black tapped a bony finger against the glass. It sounded like he was hitting it with a stone. "Down there."

Drake looked in the direction the teacher had indicated.

"Ah," said Mel. "That's cleared that up, then."

Three familiar figures leaned against a wall. They were much shorter than the kids around them, but the others were giving them a wide berth, all the same.

"They turned up this morning," Dr Black explained. "They had decided to run away, it seems, but quickly changed their minds. Nevertheless, as you can see, Mr Finn, they are very much *not* in my cupboard."

"Right, neither they are," Mel said. She caught Drake by the arm and began pulling him towards the door. "Sorry for the mix-up, glad you're not a child-killer, Dr Black. Keep it up."

"Wait." Dr Black raised a hand. "Mr Finn, I would very much like to talk to you." He glared at Mel. "In private."

Mel hesitated. She was going to argue, Drake knew. That would do neither of them any good. "It's fine," he told her, forcing a smile. "I'll catch up with you."

Reluctantly, Mel made for the door. "I'll see you in a bit," she said, and then she was gone.

Drake turned back to the window, but Dr Black was no longer there. He was sitting at his desk, his fingers loosely clasped in front of him. He indicated with a nod of his head that Drake should sit at one of the desks in the front row.

"I called for you to come to my classroom yesterday," the teacher began, once Drake was sitting down. "But you did not. Why?"

"I had a doctor's appointment."

The teacher's eyebrows arched. "Nothing serious, I trust?"

"Just a check-up."

"Ah. Very good. One can never be too careful when it comes to the subject of one's health. After all, one only lives once."

Drake remained silent.

"What would it be like, do you think? *Death*. What would death be like?"

"I don't know," Drake said. He hadn't missed the way Dr

Black had emphasised the word. "Don't really plan finding out for a while."

"Ah, but the best laid plans..." Dr Black said, leaving the rest of the sentence hanging. He began to drum his chicken-bone fingers slowly on the desktop. "The best laid plans."

The teacher stopped drumming his fingers and stared so intently that Drake feared he was looking right inside his head.

"You've taken life, though, haven't you?"

Drake was taken aback. "No," he said.

"Oh? Then perhaps your notes are mistaken. Frogs, I think they said. Didn't you burn a number of frogs to death? Wasn't that why they expelled you?"

"That was an accident!"

"A fact I'm sure the frogs were very grateful for," Dr Black continued. "As they were roasted alive."

"Look, what was it you wanted to talk to me about?" Drake asked, a little more aggressively than he had intended.

Dr Black rose slowly to his feet. "We are very alike, you and I," he said, advancing towards Drake's desk. "More alike, I think, than you realise."

"Uh, hi, Dr Black?"

Drake and the teacher both turned to find Mr Franks at the door. He was leaning into the room, a hand on each side of the doorframe. Dr Black's gums drew back into something like a snarl.

"Yes?" Dr Black said, his voice clipped. "What do you want?"

"I really need a word with Drake," Mr Franks said. "Mind if I steal him away?"

"I do indeed mind, Mr Franks. Mr Finn and I were in the middle of a conversation."

"Fine, sorry, of course. Please, carry on. I'll just wait here until you're done."

Dr Black's left eye twitched. He fixed Mr Franks with a fierce glare. When it was clear the younger teacher wasn't going to shy away, though, Dr Black turned back to Drake.

"We shall continue this another time," he glowered. "But if I catch you trespassing in my classroom again, Mr Finn, there will be grave consequences. *Grave* consequences. Is that understood?"

Drake gave a brief nod as his reply. He got to his feet, pushed the chair back in under the desk and walked, as calmly as he could, over to Mr Franks.

"Thanks, Dr Black," Mr Franks said. He stepped aside to let Drake out. "It's really important that I talk to him."

Dr Black waved a dismissive hand. "I will catch up with him again soon," he said, then he turned to the window and cast his hawk-like gaze over the school grounds below.

"I don't believe I just did that," Mr Franks muttered, as he led Drake along the corridor, away from Dr Black's room.

"Um... did what? What did you want to see me for?"

"That's just it. *Nothing*," Mr Franks said. He glanced back along the corridor and wrung his hands together nervously. "I met your friend, Mel, and she told me Dr Black was giving you trouble for something you hadn't done, and that it wasn't fair, and... well, she convinced me to come and bail you out." He shook his head. "I can't believe she talked me into it."

"She can be pretty persuasive."

Mr Franks shook his head again. His expression was still anxious, but there was a smile in there somewhere now too.

They pushed through a set of swing doors and carried on along another corridor. The further away from Dr Black's room they got, the more Drake began to relax.

"So, what did he want to see you about?" Mr Franks asked.

"Oh, you know. This and that."

"This and that," Mr Franks said. "Right. And was *this* or *that* anything to do with you cutting school yesterday? You didn't make it back to my class."

"What? Oh, no, that. I, uh, I remembered I had a doctor's appointment, that was all."

Mr Franks stopped. "Look, Drake, I don't say this often, and don't take offence, but cut the crap, OK?"

Drake blinked. "Um... what?"

"You didn't have a doctor's appointment. You cut school." He held up his hands diplomatically. "Look, you're a good kid, I can see that, and I'm sure you wouldn't duck out of school without a very good reason. You had a good reason, right?"

"Yeah," Drake said. "I did."

"Fine, right, I knew you would, but listen, Drake, don't do it again, OK? We had three kids missing yesterday, and then the accident in the car park, and then you do a runner too. It could've turned into a very difficult situation for everyone. I'm not coming on all *strict teacher* or anything, I'm just saying. You need to think about the consequences of your actions."

"Sorry," Drake mumbled. And he meant it.

"Apology accepted," the teacher said. "But, you know, if you have problems at home or whatever, or you want to talk about... anything at all, come see me, OK?" He gave Drake a firm pat on the shoulder. "We new kids have got to stick together."

CHAPTER TWENTY-ONE

A FEW HOURS later, Drake waited by the gates, watching the rest of the school file past him. No one paid him any attention, not even Bingo, Dim and Spud, the three no-longer-missing bullies. He'd felt a stirring of panic when he'd spotted them approaching, but they'd marched past in single file, none of them so much as shooting a spotty-faced sneer in his direction.

It was ten minutes since the bell had rung. Most of the other kids had left, and now only a few stragglers passed him on the way out of the gates. Drake looked up at the closest bit of the school building. The school was made up of two distinct parts. The bit at the back was a box-like construction of dull grey concrete, with evenly spaced windows that looked in danger of falling out of their frames at any moment.

In front of that was a smaller, more modern-looking extension. The outside of it was clad in weather-beaten aluminium panels, and the windows had been arranged so that, if you squinted just the right way, they almost looked like a face: three storeys of glass along the bottom, and two much larger windows like eyes up above.

Drake watched the main doors. There was a sinking feeling in his chest. Maybe Mel had already left?

He was about to start walking, when she came striding out. She half walked, half skipped over to meet him.

"Hey," he said, as she fell into step beside him.

"Hey, Chief," she smiled. "You waited for me?"

"What? Oh, no, I was just..." He shrugged. There was no point trying to hide it. "Well, yeah. Kind of. I didn't see you at lunchtime. Just wanted to make sure you were OK."

"Yeah, I was looking for you too. Did Mr Franks bail you out?"

"He did. Thanks."

"Ah, I love new teachers. So eager to be liked," she said. "What did old Blackie want?"

"He just wanted to know why I didn't go and see him yesterday, like he'd asked."

"And what did you say?"

She turned to look at him, but found the space beside her empty. Drake was standing in the middle of the pavement, several paces back. He was looking past her at the road ahead.

"You OK?"

Mel turned and followed his gaze. Further along the street, she saw a shed made of dark wood, with a jolly red roof.

"What's up?" Mel asked. "You look like you've seen a ghost."

"Can we not go this way?" Drake asked. "Is there another way to your house?"

"Lots of ways to my house," Mel said. "What's the matter, though? Is it that shed? Are you shed-o-phobic?"

"What? No."

"It's nothing to be ashamed of. Shed-o-phobia's really common. Probably."

"I'm not scared of the shed, I'd just rather—"

"Hey, look, there's someone inside," Mel said. She pointed to the door of the shed, which was now opening. A pale-faced man in a neat white suit stepped out and waved a rubber-gloved hand.

"Coo-ee! Drake!"

"Do you know that guy?" Mel asked.

Drake shook his head. "No."

"It's just that he's sort of shouting your name," Mel said. "And beckoning you over."

"He must have me mixed up with someone else," Drake said.

"Let's go and ask him," said Mel. She hooked her thumbs through the straps of her schoolbag and made her way towards the shed.

"No, wait, come back," Drake said weakly, but he knew he was wasting his breath. He had no choice but to go after her.

Pestilence was grinning from ear to ear by the time they reached the shed. "Hello, Drake," he said. He turned to Mel. "And who do we have here?"

"Mel Monday," Mel said. She held out her hand. Pestilence looked at it nervously, as if it might explode at any moment.

"He doesn't really do the handshaking thing," Drake said. "Don't take it personally."

"Very wise," Mel said. "You don't know where I might have been."

Pestilence's eyes opened a little wider. "Exactly! Ooh, I like you," he said. "What did you say your name was?"

"Mel Monday."

Pest smiled warmly. "Monday's child is fair of face," he said. "Lovely to meet you, my name's—"

"Bob," said Drake, more loudly than he had intended. Pest and Mel both turned to look at him. "Uncle Bob. He's my... He's my Uncle Bob. Isn't that right, Uncle Bob?"

"Will you hurry up?" growled a voice from inside the shed. "My back's about breaking here."

"Oh, sorry, sorry," said Pestilence. He spun a plastic arrow that was attached to a square of card in his other hand. "Left foot green."

"*Left foot green?*" War cried. "How in the name of God am I supposed to—?"

Drake reached over and pulled the door closed, and the voice became muffled. A moment later, a loud *thud* shook the wooden walls of the shed.

"What do you want, Uncle Bob?" Drake asked.

"We... thought you might like to go horse riding," Pest said. "We were going to do some practice, remember?"

This time, it was Mel's eyes that widened. "Horse riding?" she said. "Can I come?"

Pestilence suddenly looked uncomfortable. "Well, I

suppose, it's not... I mean..." He opened the shed door. "One second," he said, then he stepped inside and closed the door.

Voices muttered beyond the door. A moment later, it was yanked open, revealing a bearded giant standing inside. "You," he said, stabbing a finger at Drake. "Get in. You," he said, stabbing the same finger at Mel. "Go home."

"Maybe you can come another time?" Drake suggested, before War caught him by the arm and dragged him into the shed. "See you tomorrow!" Drake managed to cry, and then the door slammed closed between them.

"Well, she seemed *lovely*," Pest said. "But *Uncle Bob*? I mean, really? Do I look like a *Bob*? Why not Uncle Jose? Or... or... Uncle Alejandro?"

"What do you think you're doing?" Drake demanded, glaring at War. "You can't just go dragging me in here any time you feel like it."

"And you can't go shirking your duties any time you feel like it. We let you go home last night on the understanding you met us after school. It's now after school, so we saved you the bother of coming to us."

Drake crossed his arms over his chest and looked away. For the first time since entering the shed, he spotted Famine.

He was lying face down on a *Twister* mat, apparently unconscious.

"Right, fine," Drake scowled. "Where are we going?"

Pestilence slipped a slim remote control into his breast pocket. "We're already there," he said, and he opened the door.

Drake didn't recognise the field at first. It wasn't until he spotted the narrow river, and the bridge that the floating sphere had hidden behind, that he knew where he was.

"What are we doing here?" he asked, following War and Pestilence outside. Famine, for the moment, remained unconscious.

"Like I said, horse riding," Pest told him.

Drake swept his gaze across the field. "Won't we need horses for that?"

"We most certainly will. That's the first part of the lesson, actually."

"What do you mean?"

War stepped between them. He curved his middle finger and thumb into the shape of a letter C and stuck them in his mouth. A shrill whistle almost made Drake's eardrums burst.

"Bloody Hell," he cried, clamping his hands over his ears.

"Tell me when you're going to do that, will you?"

Even through his hands, Drake heard the thunderclap. It rolled across the field, bending the grass and swirling the surface of the river. The force of it made Drake take a step backwards. Pestilence, who had clearly been expecting it, took shelter behind War.

"Did you... Did you just whistle for thunder?" Drake asked.

"Only gods can make thunder," War told him. "I just whistled for *him*."

"Who?" Drake asked, before a horse leaped from thin air and sailed over his head. He turned and watched it gallop across the field for a few hundred metres, gradually slowing down. Shortly before it slowed to a full stop, it turned and began cantering back towards them. Drake watched its mane dance like fire in the afternoon sun.

"Oh, great," he muttered, as the red horse *clopped* closer. "You again."

Another piercing whistle sent him ducking for cover. He looked up to see Pestilence take both pinkie fingers out of his mouth.

"Seriously, will you *please* give me some warning before

you do that?" Drake cried, but another boom of thunder drowned him out before the sentence was even half finished.

This time Drake was ready for the wind. He ducked his head and angled his body to avoid being shoved back. When he looked up, the front half of a white horse was slouching towards him. The back half followed a moment later. Drake saw the air round the horse ripple, as if the world itself had parted, just for a moment, to let the animal through.

The horse kept walking until it reached Pestilence. "You can pat him, if you like," Pest said encouragingly.

Drake looked up at the horse. It was almost as big as War's. Whereas the red horse looked like it should be put on display by an art gallery, though, this one looked like it should be put down by a vet.

Weeping sores dotted the horse's flanks, and a dark crimson liquid dripped from within its mouth and round its eyes. Its tail and mane were ragged and filthy. As it walked, Drake could see every one of its ribs beneath its dry, shrivelled skin.

The horse whinnied loudly, but the whinny became a cough and the cough, eventually, became a raspy wheeze. The animal limped over to stand beside War's horse, which promptly took two paces in the opposite direction.

"Um... is your horse OK?" Drake asked, as diplomatically as he could. "It looks a bit, sort of, under the weather."

"Don't let his appearance fool you," Pestilence said. "He's fit as a fiddle, that one. Aren't you, love?"

The horse neighed, retched, then vomited on to the grass. "Fit as a fiddle," Pestilence repeated, somewhat less confidently.

"Now it's your turn," War said.

"My turn for what?"

"Summon your steed. Call forth the pale horse," War told him.

Drake nodded uncertainly. "How do I do that?"

"You whistle," snapped War, whose patience was rapidly approaching wafer-thinness. "Like we did."

"I can't whistle."

War stared. A breeze blew. Pest's horse suffered spectacular diarrhoea.

"*What* did you say?"

"I said I can't whistle. Is that a problem?"

War's teeth clamped together until there was barely room for the words to escape. "Yes," he growled. "That's a problem.

If you can't whistle, how can you call your horse?"

"I dunno, can't I just shout or something?"

"And what would you shout, exactly?"

"Sort of, 'Here, horsey horsey,' or something," Drake suggested. "Would that work?"

War shook his head. "No," he said, in a voice like two bricks rubbing together. "That wouldn't work."

"Can you try whistling?" Pestilence asked. "You just sort of stick your fingers in your mouth and blow. It's not that difficult."

"I've tried before," Drake said. He stuck his fingers in his mouth and blew, as Pest had suggested. What came out sounded almost exactly like the white horse's last bowel movement. "See? Can't do it."

"No, you can't, can you?" Pest said glumly.

"I can whistle normally. A bit," Drake said. He pursed his lips together and made a warbly, high-pitched squeak. "That any use?"

"Oh, aye, that'll be very handy if we ever need to summon a budgie," War spat.

"Keep practising and it'll come," Pestilence said encouragingly.

"And what do you suggest we do in the meantime?" War asked.

Pestilence looked up and squinted in the glare of the sun. "It's a lovely day," he said brightly. "What's say we go for a ride?"

CHAPTER TWENTY-TWO

THE GROUND ROLLED by in a blur beneath the horse's hooves. Despite appearances, Pestilence's horse was strong. It galloped across the fields and bounded over fences, matching the pace of War's mount without any sign of difficulty.

On its back, Pestilence clutched the reins. Drake sat behind him, holding on to a handle at the rear of the saddle, and silently praying that the horse wouldn't go airborne.

"You OK back there?" Pest asked.

"Well, I haven't fallen off yet," Drake replied.

Pestilence smiled. "That's a good start." He was holding the reins with one hand. With the other, he was applying a thick white cream to his face. "Got to put this stuff on or I'll blister something terrible in this sun," he explained. "I got so burned last time I looked like I'd been bobbing for chips."

"Shouldn't you, you know, see a doctor?" Drake asked him.

"For sunburn?"

"For everything. It's just, you seem to have a few medical... issues."

The horse leaped over a small stone wall. Pestilence waited for it to touch back down before he replied. "Comes with the job, don't it? Pestilence means plague and disease and viruses and stuff. That's me all over, that. And it's not exactly a barrel of laughs, let me tell you."

"Is that why you wear the gloves and stuff? So you can try and avoid catching germs?"

"More the other way round," Pest explained. "I can't catch anything from humans, but there's no saying what they might catch from me."

Drake subtly slid himself further back in the seat. "Relax," Pest laughed. "You're not human any more."

"*What?* Well, what am I, then?"

"You're a Horseman of the Apocalypse, of course." Pestilence paused a moment, letting this information sink in. "Well, for the next ninety days, anyway."

"What happens after ninety days?" Drake asked.

Pestilence smiled, but Drake couldn't see it. "You're going to quit, remember?"

"Oh, yeah. So I am," Drake nodded. "Is Famine going to be OK?"

"Hmm? Oh, he'll be fine. Just over-exerted himself a bit. Best to let him sleep it off."

Up ahead, War's horse cleared a five-metre-wide stream in a single leap. Pest slipped his suncream into his jacket pocket and gave the reins a flick. Drake felt the ground fall away as the horse jumped. It seemed to hang in mid-air for several seconds, before landing on the opposite bank with a jarring jolt.

"What's my horse like?" Drake asked. He had to admit, he was a little disappointed he hadn't been able to summon it.

"No idea," Pestilence replied. "Every Death has had a different horse. Yours doesn't exist yet. It won't exist until you summon it."

"War keeps saying I'm the rider on the pale horse, though."

"Just a Bible quotation," Pest shrugged. "I think the first Death's horse was a sort of sickly green colour, but there's been all sorts since then. Death Eight's horse was made of living magma. Used to ruin his trousers whenever he sat on it." Pest sighed sadly. "No wonder the poor beggar killed himself. The goldfish had a lime-green one, if I remember right."

"The goldfish had a horse?" Drake gaped. "What, you mean even *it* could whistle?"

"After a fashion," Pest said. "If you squeezed it hard enough."

"You didn't!"

"Of course the goldfish didn't have a horse," laughed the horseman. "It borrowed mine. But anyway, the point is your horse might be pale, or it might be bright purple, we'll just have to wait and see. War just likes his Bible quotes."

"I don't think he likes me," Drake said.

There was a lengthy pause before Pestilence spoke again. "He doesn't like anyone. Not really. And he's... not convinced you're a suitable choice for Death."

"And what do you think?"

"I think we could've done a lot worse."

"Thanks," Drake said. "But what if he's right? What if there's been a mistake? Maybe I'm not supposed to be Death."

"The powers that be don't make mistakes," Pest assured him.

"What about the goldfish?"

"The powers that be don't make mistakes *very often*. That was a one-off."

Drake stayed quiet for a while after that. The horses galloped across the wide fields, racing up the hills and thundering down the dales. Despite the blinding speed and the nagging worry that he could fall off at any moment, Drake actually found himself enjoying the journey.

A suspicion had been nagging at him for the past few hours, though, and Pestilence had been pretty forthcoming with information so far.

"The old Death," he said. "Death Nine. What did he look like?"

"A sort of big, black wraith figure. Like a living version of the Robe of Sorrows, if you can imagine such a thing."

"Oh, right," said Drake, a little disappointed. "Not a skinny old man with a big hooked nose, then?"

"Ah, you mean what did he look like in human form?" Pest asked. "Dark and sinister, probably, but that's just a guess. We never got to see him. He wasn't human when he started."

"What was he?"

"Just an ominous black shape, really. We've had a few

Deaths like that. God knows where they get them."

"But he definitely turned human when he left?" Drake asked.

"Oh, yes. That's in the contract, that. Terminate the agreement in any way and you'll take human form, regardless of what form you might've been to begin with."

"War said that he could do it. The old Death, I mean. That he could bring on Armageddon."

Pestilence spoke hesitantly. "He said he *might* be able to do it, but only if he'd planned things well in advance."

"The robotic demon in the Junk Room, and the sphere things at school," Drake said quietly. "They must've been planned in advance, right?"

"Yes," Pest admitted. "I'd think they must have."

"How will we know if he does do it?"

"We'll get a phone call. And, of course, there'll be signs."

"What kind of signs?" asked Drake.

Pest shrugged. "Oh, the usual. Earthquakes. Raining blood. Plagues of locusts. That sort of thing."

He gave another flick of the reins and the horse bounded over the remains of an old stone cottage.

"They've got this book, see? Them upstairs. The Book

of Everything. It tells them... well, it tells them *everything*, like you might expect. But most importantly, as far as we're concerned, it tells them when the end of the world is coming, so they can start rolling out the signs. It's a pretty foolproof system."

War's horse slowed to a stop and the giant leaped down on to the grass. Pest brought his own horse to a halt beside him. The animal broke wind loudly.

"Ooh, better out than in!" laughed Pestilence.

With a hoarse hacking sound, the horse coughed blood on to the grass.

"Probably better in than out, that one," Pest said weakly. He swung his leg down into an expert dismount. He and War watched as Drake slid awkwardly in the saddle, kicked frantically in mid-air, then landed in a heap on the ground.

"Aw, smoothly done," War said, clapping his hands together slowly.

Drake stood up and tried to brush the grass stains from his trousers. They smudged a little, but didn't go away. Mum wasn't going to be happy about that.

"Yeah, very funny. What did you stop for?" Drake asked.

"Last night you asked about Death's abilities," War intoned.

"I thought now might be a good time to discuss them."

Drake looked at the wide-open space around them. Aside from a small tin shack at the foot of one of the hills, there was nothing in any direction but fields and trees and dirt-track roads.

"Out here?"

"Yes, out here, where there's less chance of you accidentally killing anyone."

Drake's stomach went tight. "I'm not killing anyone," he said quickly. "Is that what I'm supposed to do? I'm not doing that."

"*Accidentally* killing anyone, I said," War growled. "No one's asking you to kill anyone on purpose."

"But isn't that what I do, though?" Drake asked. He was suddenly realising exactly what he might have got himself into. "I mean, if I'm Death, that's what I do, right?" He clamped a hand over his mouth. "Oh my God, I'm evil, aren't I? Death, War, Famine, Pestilence; we're all evil!"

"No one has to kill anyone," Pestilence explained. "All we're supposed to do is ride the horses across the sky come Judgement Day. We're like *mascots*, really. Just sort of cutting the ribbon to declare Armageddon open for business."

"And we're not evil," War said. His nostrils were flared in a sneer, as if the very suggestion offended him. "Wars can lead to freedom. A plague or a famine have no will of their own, they're natural events."

"But what about me?" Drake asked quietly. "Death's evil, isn't it?"

"Murder's evil," War said. "But death? No. Death can be the end of suffering. Death can be a welcome visitor. I have seen people begging for death, and weeping with relief when it finally came. Most people fear death, but sometimes, in the end, it's the only friend they've got."

"And on that cheerful note," said Pest, doing his best to ease the tension, "let's get on with the training!"

Drake rapped his knuckles against the side of the tin hut. *Clang, clang, clang.* He turned to War. "You want me to do *what*?"

War sighed. "Enter the shack."

"But not through the door?"

"No, not through the door. What would be the point in that? 'Here's your third challenge – walk through a door.' No, I don't think so."

Drake studied the wall of the hut again. It was made of a heavy corrugated iron, rusted in patches, but still completely solid.

"But I can't walk through the wall," Drake said. "I mean, it's impossible."

"To Drake Finn, maybe, but not to Death," War explained. "Death can go anywhere. Nothing can hold it out, not distance, not magic and certainly not a rusty sheet of metal."

"It's a belief thing," Pestilence said encouragingly. "*I* believe you can do it. The question is – do you?"

"No," said Drake, shaking his head. "I don't."

"Go on, give it a try," said Pest. "I bet you'll be a natural."

Drake looked doubtful. He brushed a hand against the metal. It still felt solid.

"OK, I'll try," he said, prompting a short burst of excited applause from Pestilence.

Taking two paces back, Drake lined himself up with the side of the metal shack. He straightened his back, held his head high and closed his eyes.

"Here goes," he muttered, then he took one pace, two paces, thr—

THUD.

Drake opened his eyes. His face was pressed against the side of the shack.

"Oh, aye, a natural," War snorted.

"It's impossible," Drake insisted. "I can't do it."

"Because you didn't believe you could," War said. "You shuffled up there like you were queuing for your pension. You were just waiting to hit the wall."

"Of course I was!" Drake snapped. "I knew I was going to."

"You don't get it, do you?" War roared. Startled by the sound, a flock of nearby birds took to the air in panic. "There *is* no wall! Not to you! Nothing can keep you out!"

He pointed to a spot some ten metres away from the shack. "Get over there," he growled. "Take a run up at it, don't slow down, just pretend it's not there and you'll sail right through."

"But—"

"*Now!*" War bellowed. Drake could tell from the way the veins were standing out on the giant's forehead that he probably shouldn't argue. He walked over to the spot and turned to face the hut. It suddenly looked to be a long way away.

"Right, now run," War barked. "Fast as you can."

"Fast as I can," Drake said. "Right."

He sprang forward like a sprinter off the blocks, his hands

bunched tightly into fists.

"You can do it, Drake," he heard Pest cry, and then he was past the other horsemen, powering on, throwing himself at full speed at the rigid metal barrier...

A flash of panic filled his head. *Rigid metal barrier.*

He hit it shoulder-first and his whole skeleton shook with the impact. There was a sharp squeal that Drake at first thought must be Pestilence, but then the wall collapsed, and Drake's momentum carried him through on top of it.

There was more squealing from the other walls as the metal tore, and they slowly folded in like a house of cards on top of him.

Drake didn't think he could feel any pain, but he couldn't be entirely sure. He lay there, just in case, pinned beneath the corrugated iron. Eventually, a pair of powerful hands lifted the walls away.

"Well, that was one way to get inside," Pestilence said, smiling cheerfully. "But maybe we should try something else?"

Drake looked down at his school uniform. It was stained with patches of orange, where it had come into contact with the rust. His shoulder throbbed where it had connected with the metal. More than that, though, there was another sensation niggling at him. Shame. He was embarrassed by his performance. Behind War's beard, Drake was sure the giant was laughing.

He looked up and saw that the sky overhead was slowly darkening.

"No more training," he said. "I want to go home."

The veins on War's head stood out again, but he didn't shout this time. Instead, he stomped past Drake and swung himself up into the saddle of his ruby red horse. "I tell you," he muttered, "this ninety days can't end soon enough."

With a "*Yah!*" and a tug of the reins, War and his horse took to the sky and were quickly lost among the clouds.

"He doesn't mean it," said Pest softly.

Drake sniffed. "I don't care," he said. "Just take me home."

CHAPTER TWENTY-THREE

DRAKE LAY IN bed, listening to the ticking of his clock. He'd stopped looking at it a few hours ago, when the hands had been creeping past one o'clock. No matter how hard he'd tried since then, he couldn't fall asleep.

He put it down to worry. He could never sleep when he was worried, and right now things were queuing up to be worried about.

Someone was trying to kill him. Someone *had* tried to kill him. Twice. That was one of the things bothering him, but that wasn't even the biggie.

Armageddon. The end of the world. It sounded ridiculous – the idea that the whole world could just suddenly and abruptly come to a stop. How could one man destroy the whole world and everyone on it? It seemed impossible.

And yet both Pestilence and War had said it *was* possible. And, of course, Death Nine wasn't just any normal man.

Drake thought about that. The old Death was human now – someone 'dark and sinister' if Pestilence was right. That pointed to one obvious suspect. And the metal sphere *had* come from inside his classroom.

Could Dr Black be the old Death? Drake had been relieved when Mr Franks showed up to take him away from the history teacher's classroom, but now he couldn't help but wonder what he might have found out if he'd hung around.

The cupboard, he thought, might still hold some answers, even if it didn't hold the bodies of Bingo and his cohorts. It was worth a look, anyway. He'd have to find some way of unlocking the door, of course, but maybe there'd be something in there to help him figure out if Dr Black really was Death number nine. And, if he was, maybe there'd be some sort of clue as to whether he really was capable of ending the world.

Drake rolled over, making the bed creak. A few nights ago he'd been lying awake worrying about starting school.

Now he was lying awake worrying about the Apocalypse. A lot had happened since Monday.

Drake got up, tiptoed to the window and looked out. Through the darkness, he could just make out a small red roof at the far end of the garden.

Pulling on a jumper and wriggling his feet into his shoes, Drake undid the window latch, and quietly slid the wooden frame open.

Famine was sitting on the grass outside the shed, his back leaning against a side wall. He looked up as Drake approached, revealing a face smeared with streaks of brown. The fat man's fingers dipped into a jar of chocolate spread he held between his thighs. He scooped out a dollop of the stuff, licked the finger clean, then clamped a pudgy hand over the jar.

"It's mine," he said.

"Yeah, I know," Drake said. "I'm not hungry, anyway."

"Lucky you," Famine replied, as he scooped out some more of the gooey spread.

Drake sat on the grass beside him. "I couldn't sleep," he said. "Thought some fresh air might help."

"It won't," Famine said. "You don't need as much sleep now. Hardly any, really."

"Really? I don't know if that's good or bad," Drake admitted.

"Bad," Famine told him. "Very bad. Being awake's overrated."

Drake thought about this. "I suppose you could get lots done, though, without sleep."

"Maybe. If you had something worth doing," Famine said. "All we have to do is wait. You don't need to be awake to wait."

He reached the bottom of the jar. Drake watched in horrified fascination as the horseman stuck his tongue into the container and began licking the inside clean.

"You're doing the right thing, I reckon," Famine said, when the jar was spotless.

"What do you mean?"

"Jacking it in. We've been waiting on the call for what, six or seven thousand years now? Starting to drag a bit, if I'm being honest. You're best getting out when you can."

"How come you've all lasted?" Drake asked. "Why is it just Death that keeps –" he reached for a suitable word, but couldn't find one – "cracking up?"

Famine shrugged. The shed he was leaning against creaked loudly in protest. "Death's the leader, and he's the most powerful. Maybe it's that that does it. The power. Or maybe it's the responsibility. Don't ask me."

"The most powerful?" Drake muttered. "I can't even summon my horse."

"You'll get there. It just takes practice. And the right mindset."

"And the ability to whistle," Drake added.

Famine grunted what might have been a laugh. "Yeah, that's a help an' all." He lifted up a roll of flab and pulled out a tin of mackerel. "You really can't whistle?" he asked, cracking the ring pull and tearing open the lid.

Drake put his fingers in his mouth and blew. A slightly damp silence emerged. "Nope," he said. "I've never been able to do it."

Famine lifted the can to his lips and half drank, half ate the fishy contents. Drake thought that it was just as well he wasn't hungry. After that, he didn't think he'd ever want to eat again.

"What's your horse like?" Drake asked, when Famine had

wiped the oily fish residue from his chin.

"Bandy-legged," Famine said, then he laughed a hollow laugh. "I don't ride much, these days." He looked at his hands, all smeared with oil and fish bits. "Don't do much of anything, these days."

They sat in silence for a while longer. "I think... I mean, I'm not sure, but I think one of my teachers might be Death. The old Death, I mean. The last one."

"Oh?"

"Yeah. Dr Black, his name is. Do you think he could be?"

Famine shrugged. "Why don't you ask him?"

"Well, because he might try to kill me again, for one thing."

"Yeah, he might at that. Still, I suppose it'll all be over soon."

Drake frowned. "What do you mean?"

"The Apocalypse. If he kicks it all off, it'll all be over for everyone. Won't have to worry about anything any more."

Drake thought about this. "Yeah. I suppose."

He got to his feet. There was a strong breeze blowing around the garden, and he was surprised he didn't feel cold. "I'm going to head back to bed and lie awake until morning."

"Sounds like a plan," Famine said.

Drake gave him a nod. "See you later."

"See you later."

Drake was almost at the wall of weeds when he stopped. "Do you mind if I ask you something?"

Famine shook his head. "I don't mind."

"Why don't you quit? If you don't like it, why don't you quit?"

"Look at me," Famine said. He gestured down at himself in general. "What else could I do?"

Drake didn't quite know what to say to that, so he smiled in what he hoped was a supportive way. "Bye, then," he said, and he pushed aside the first few blades of the tangled grass.

"G'night, Drake."

With one final glance back, Drake slipped into the grass and headed for home.

"How was horse riding?"

The question accosted Drake before he had reached the end of the path. Mel popped up from behind the fence. Drake couldn't help noticing that her hair was a shocking shade of red.

"Um... it didn't really work out in the end," he told her. "Don't think it's my strong point."

"Shame," said Mel, but Drake thought she looked secretly quite pleased by this news. "Maybe I can teach you one day."

"Yeah, that would be... What happened to your hair?"

"Oh that; like it? I'm in disguise."

"What as? A tomato?"

"Hey, that was quite quick for you," she said, smiling. "No, I'm disguised as someone with red hair." She explained it slowly, as if talking to an idiot. "So, you know, someone who's not me."

Drake hopped over the gate. "And why are you in disguise, exactly?"

"Because I don't want to be recognised when we sneak back into Dr Black's classroom," she explained.

"And why are we doing that?" Drake asked. Even though he'd had exactly the same idea himself, he was interested to hear Mel's reason for it.

"Because I was thinking – he still lied. Whether Bingo and that lot turned up or not, he still lied about you being the last one to see them. So, after you went into the shed with your uncle – which, you know, is a new level of weird, by the way – I went back to the school and watched for Dr Black coming out."

"And?" Drake asked.

"He didn't."

"He didn't what?"

"He didn't come out. I stood there until ten o'clock. He didn't come out."

Drake raised both eyebrows in surprise. "Ten o'clock? Seriously?"

"Wasn't like I had anything better to do," Mel said. "After that, I went straight home and disguised my head. He's up to something, I'm sure of it, and we need to find out what."

Drake bit his tongue, then decided just to go for it. "I think he's going to try to destroy the world."

Mel looked back at him blankly.

"I mean, I'm not sure, but he might be."

"Right," she said slowly. "Because I was thinking he might be sleeping in his classroom or something. Like, maybe he couldn't pay his rent."

"Or it could be that," Drake backpedalled. "It could be that too."

Mel considered the alternatives. "Either one's reason enough to snoop around in the cupboard, I reckon." She made up her mind. "If he's planning on destroying the world, then we'll stop him. If he's using the cupboard to sleep in then we'll, I don't know, fart on his bed or something. Deal?"

"Deal," said Drake, then he drew in a breath. "Imagine he *was* planning to destroy the world," he said. He tried to sound like he was joking, but his voice took on a serious tone all by itself. "What if we couldn't stop him? What if no one could?"

Mel thought about this. "That," she announced, at last, "would be a real bummer."

CHAPTER TWENTY-FOUR

THIS TIME, THEY waited until lunch before going anywhere near Dr Black's classroom. He was on guard duty at the canteen, making sure the food didn't incite anyone to riot. This meant he would be out of the way for at least twenty-five minutes. That left plenty of time for Drake and Mel to snoop around.

The cupboard door, however, was still locked. Drake studied it. He tapped the wood in several places, without having any real idea why. He'd seen them do it in DIY shows on TV before, so presumably it must serve some purpose.

"I suppose I could try walking through it," he said. One of the good things about Mel, he had discovered, was that he could say almost anything he wanted to her, and she never seemed in the least bit surprised. Like just then, for example.

"You could try that, certainly," she said. She held up a key. "Or, we could try this."

Drake's eyes lit up. "Where did you get that?"

"Like I said, I have my sources. Don't ask too many questions," she said mysteriously. Then she added, "It was there. On the desk."

"Oh," said Drake, a little disappointed. If there really *was* something sinister in the cupboard, Dr Black was unlikely to leave the key just lying around for anyone to find. "Give it a try, then," he urged.

Mel slid the key into the lock. There was a soft *clunk* as it turned. Mel pushed the door open and a cool breeze hit them both in the face. From within the cupboard, Drake heard the low drone of an air-conditioning system, and a feeling of dread began to pump through his veins.

"Mel, wait," he said, but Mel was already stepping into the darkened space and fumbling for the light switch. He bounded in after her as the light came on, revealing a room just two metres wide, and about three times as long.

The cupboard was completely empty, aside from a table that took up almost the entire length of the back wall. A black cloth covered the table and hung down to the floor on all sides. On top of the tablecloth were tools and circuit boards and oddly shaped pieces of metal. Above it, bolted on to the ceiling, two fans noisily pumped out cold air.

Mel raced up to the table and began prodding at the circuit boards. Drake was more cautious. The fans were just like those in the Junk Room cave. He kept his eyes open for self-assembly robotic demons as he walked over to join her.

"I don't believe I'm seeing this," said a voice from behind them. Drake and Mel turned to find Mr Franks in the doorway of the cupboard. He had his arms folded across his chest and an expression that was halfway between disappointed and furious. "What are you doing here?" he demanded. "You shouldn't be in here."

Mel was talking before an excuse could form in Drake's head.

"I'm glad you're here, Mr Franks," she said. "Something fishy's going on."

"You're breaking into Dr Black's cupboard. That's what's fishy," the teacher said reproachfully.

"No, check this out," Mel said, indicating the circuitry and components on the tabletop. "Tell me this isn't weird stuff for a history teacher to have lying around?"

Despite himself, Mr Franks peered past them. He cast his gaze across the items on the table.

"What is that stuff?" he asked, staying back by the door. "You shouldn't be messing about with it. Dr Black wouldn't like it."

"No," Mel said. She gave a low whistle. "He probably wouldn't. What do you think it is?"

Drake studied the bits of metal. He didn't recognise any of them, although he recognised their shiny chrome colour. "Not sure," he said, only half lying.

Mr Franks took a few faltering steps into the cupboard and looked down over their shoulders. "It's probably nothing," he said. "Just... some sort of project, or something."

"Yeah, Project *Destroy the World*," Mel said dramatically. "Or Project Build a Home Computer in Sixty Collectable Parts. One or the other."

"It's not like any computer I've ever seen," Mr Franks said. Despite his initial concerns about them being in the cupboard, he couldn't help but be interested by the components on the table. He picked up a circuit board and studied it. "It looks so... advanced," he said. "Where did he get his hands on something like this?"

"You could ask him," suggested Mel.

"Ha," said Mr Franks, without humour. "Yeah, there's an idea."

Mel swallowed and pointed to the cupboard door. "No, I mean, *you could ask him*."

Mr Franks and Drake both set down the components they were holding, and turned round. The skeletal frame of Dr Black stood in the doorway, his face drawn in anger.

"What... do you think... you are doing?" he demanded in a voice like grinding teeth.

"Dr Black, there you are," Mr Franks said. He walked towards the other teacher, trying to smile, but failing miserably. "I can explain; you see we were—"

The back of Dr Black's hand caught Mr Franks across the side of the face. The younger teacher spun until he hit the closest wall. With a faint whimper, he slid down the wall and on to the lino floor.

"Whoa," Mel said. For the first time since Drake had met her, she looked genuinely shocked. "That was harsh."

Dr Black took a step into the cupboard. Behind him, the door swung closed. "Mr Finn. Miss Monday," he said, over-pronouncing every syllable. "I told you not to come here again. I warned you to stay away, but yet here you are, trying to interfere with my plans." He took another step towards them. "Do you think you can stop me? Is that it? Don't you realise the irony? It isn't your job to try to stop me. It's *your* job to stand at the sidelines and cheer me on."

"You *are* him," Drake said. He'd had his suspicions, but having them confirmed still came as a shock. "You're Death Nine."

"At your service," Dr Black said, bowing his head just slightly.

"Death Nine? What are you talking about?" Mel asked.

"The others told me why you left. What are you planning to do?" Drake asked. He couldn't hide the tremble in his voice.

"First, I'm going to get my strength back. And then I'm going to do something –" he waved a hand around, as if searching for a fitting word – "spectacular."

"Like what?"

Dr Black gave a low chuckle. "I'm not a Bond villain, Mr Finn. Do you really think I'm going to tell you every detail of my scheme?"

"Well, I kind of hoped..."

"I *will* tell you when I'm going to put it into action, though. When I'm going to start the ball rolling on Armageddon, so to speak."

"When?"

Dr Black reached into his pocket and pulled out a sleek black smartphone. He swiped a finger across the screen a few times, then stabbed a thumb against one of the icons.

"Armageddon," Dr Black said, with a callous smile. "There's an app for that."

"What did you do?" Drake demanded. "What have you done?"

"I've started the ball rolling on the end of the world, but you shouldn't concern yourself with what I've done. You should worry about what I'm *going* to do next." He leaned in closer. "I'm going to kill you, Mr Finn. Right now. And after I've killed you, I'm going to kill her." He shifted his gaze to Mel for just a second, but in that moment, Drake saw his chance.

Roaring, he threw himself at the teacher, shoulder lowered, chin tucked into his chest. War had said that in human form the previous Death would be powerless. He looked frail too. One solid hit should be enough to take him down.

Drake ploughed into Dr Black, but it felt like he'd run head-first into a wall. The teacher didn't so much as take a single backwards step. He caught the bent-over boy by the waist, hoisted him into the air, then smashed him back down on the floor beside Mr Franks. Drake was surprised – not by the unexpected wrestling move, although that was surprising enough in itself. He was more surprised by the fact that it didn't really hurt.

It also didn't hurt when the tip of Dr Black's shoe was driven into his ribs, although he definitely felt it. Drake rolled clumsily in the narrow cupboard and scrambled to get back to his feet.

"Hey, leave him alone!" Mel yelled. She moved to lash out at the teacher, but Drake's arm came up to block her way.

"Don't," he said sharply. "Stay away from him. He'll kill you. He's crazy."

Two pinpricks of red lit up in the teacher's eyes. "You say the sweetest things."

"What's going on?" Mel asked, backing away.

"Tell her, Mr Finn," Dr Black oozed. "Tell her everything. Tell her what you really are."

"What's he talking about?" The usual light-hearted tone

was gone from Mel's voice now. She was serious. And she was scared. "What have you got me mixed up in?"

"I'll explain later," said Drake. "I promise."

"You know, Mr Finn," Dr Black began. He raised his bony hands in a choking motion. "You really shouldn't make promises that you cannot keep."

THUDOOM!

The door at Dr Black's back flew open with such force that it cracked the solid stone wall where it hit. The teacher spun one-eighty on his toes, his hands now clenched into fists.

At first, he saw no one, but a movement down by the floor soon caught his attention. He looked down to see a flea-ridden creature glaring back up at him. The hair on the cat's back stood up as it bared its rotten teeth, extended its filthy claws and said, "Woof".

CHAPTER TWENTY-FIVE

A SHORT DISTANCE away, in a dark wooden shed in an overgrown back garden, a telephone rang. It was the first time, since time itself had begun, that this particular telephone had made a sound.

The three men sitting at the table tensed. War straightened his shoulders, adjusted his sword, then smoothed down his beard. Only then did he reach for the receiver and listen to the clipped tones of the person on the other end of the line.

"Yes, sir," he said eventually. "I understand, sir."

With a *click*, War hung up the phone. He undid the laces of his boots, then tied them again, tighter this time. Only then did he look at the other men.

"Right, then," he said, with an uncharacteristic tremor in his voice. "That's us."

✦

Drake looked down at the barking cat and couldn't contain his delight. "Toxie!"

"Hey! It's that ca—" said Mel, before Drake's hand clamped over her mouth.

"Don't say it," he warned.

Dr Black's lips drew up into a mirthless grin. "Nice kitty," he said, then he toe-punted the mangy animal across the room. It clattered hard against the bottom of a bookcase. The shelves wobbled back and forth, back and forth, and then they toppled forward, showering Toxie in hardback history books, before crunching down on top of him.

The teacher returned his attention to his captive audience. "Now," he said. "Where were we?"

There was a sudden *boom* and the bookcase exploded. A shape, like a small cat becoming a big something else, glowed white hot in the corner of the classroom.

The three still-conscious occupants of the cupboard watched as Toxie's back tore open, and a row of spiky plates grew from his spine. His stubby bones snapped and splintered, then joined together again in new shapes and new sizes. A hide of molten granite burned through the tattered remains of his fur, as the slender muscles across his shoulders bulged. In just a few seconds, Toxie's body had become that of a terrifying Hellhound.

His head, though, was still very much a cat.

"Getting there," said Drake encouragingly.

Toxie wagged his forked tail and *woofed* happily.

"What the Hell is going on?" Mel asked, catching Drake by the sleeve and not letting go.

"I'll explain that later too. But for now, you might want to step back."

He put himself in front of Mel just as Toxie's powerful back legs twitched. The Hellhound bounded on to Dr Black's desk, his paws leaving scorch-marks on the wood. Dr Black's twisted grin didn't falter.

"Here, kitty, kitty," he growled, beckoning the monster over. Toxie's tiny jaws opened wide as he hurled himself at the history teacher. Dr Black twisted to the side, raised his arm in front of his chest, then drove his elbow into the Hellhound's throat.

Toxie's momentum carried him forward, regardless. Dr Black turned and bent low as the full weight of the snarling Hellhound landed on his back. Incredibly, he didn't fall.

Even more incredibly, he straightened back up in one jerky movement.

"Bad kitty," he said, then he ran backwards out of the cupboard. Drake and Mel watched him charge across the classroom, dodging desks and chairs, the Hellhound howling with fury on his back.

And then there was a loud *KRIK* as Dr Black drove the beast against the wall. A spider's web pattern spread up the plaster and Toxie let out a squeal of pain. Dr Black glared into the cupboard and fixed his eyes on Drake. He began to cackle, quietly at first, but quickly becoming louder until the sound of his laughter drowned out Toxie's yelps.

"We should get out of here," Drake muttered.

"You think?" Mel said. She took hold of Drake's hand and he led her out into the classroom. "What do we do about him?" she asked, glancing back at the unconscious Mr Franks.

Drake thought for a moment, then firmly pulled the cupboard door closed. "He'll be fine," he said. "Probably."

"Where do you think you are going, Mr Finn?" Dr Black demanded. He made a lunge for them, but Toxie dug his claws into the teacher's shoulders and dropped to the floor. Dr Black was pulled backwards.

"Go, go, go," Drake cried, pushing Mel towards the classroom door. They clattered out into the corridor and slammed the door closed, muffling the sounds of the battle raging inside.

"That was... What was...?" Mel stammered. She shook her head and pulled herself together. "What's happening?"

"I'll explain soon, I promise," he said. "But now we have to run."

He caught her hand again and pulled her along the corridor towards the exit. Pupils usually didn't bother going upstairs during breaktimes, so the history corridor was completely deserted. Their footsteps echoed noisily as they made for the corner that led to the stairs.

Drake skidded round the bend, dragging Mel with him. Three figures blocked the top of the stairs. They turned their spotty faces Drake's way as he appeared round the corner.

"Well, well, well, if it ain't the knob 'ead," Bingo muttered. "Been eating any Frosties lately?"

"Not now, guys, OK?" Drake said. He moved to pass them, but Dim and Spud blocked his way.

"We've been looking for you," Bingo continued.

"No, you haven't," Drake said. "You walked right past me yesterday."

"Yeah, well now we are looking for you, all right? Did you think we forgot what you done?"

There was a *crash* from along the corridor behind them. None of the three bullies so much as blinked.

"I'm warning you, get out of my way," Drake said. "We need to get out of here. All of us."

"You ain't going nowhere, knob 'ead." Bingo looked Mel up and down. He fixed his eyes on her checked skirt and leered. "And neither's your girlfriend."

Bingo made a grab for Mel, both hands raised, fingers spread wide. Drake let go of her hand long enough to shove the bully in the chest. "Leave her alone," he yelled, in a voice that didn't sound quite like his own.

In his panicked rage, Drake pushed the boy harder than he had intended. He watched helplessly as Bingo stumbled back towards the stairs. The bully's face barely had time to register his surprise before he started to fall.

All four of them looked on, dumbstruck, as Bingo clattered down the hard stone steps. He bounced and rolled down the last few stairs and hit the floor below with a sickening *crunch*.

In the silence that followed, Drake was deafened by the thunder of his own crashing heart.

Mel looked down at the motionless boy, lying on his back, his limbs bent at awkward angles. Both shaking hands went to her mouth. "Oh God," she whispered. "Oh God."

"What have I done?" Drake whimpered. "He's not moving. What have I done?"

Dim and Spud kept quiet. They followed Drake and Mel as they hurried down the stairs.

"I've... I've killed him," Drake said. "I've actually killed him."

"Maybe not," Mel said. "I mean, maybe not. There's no blood or anything."

"No, but..." Drake remembered the crunching sound Bingo had made on the floor, and the way his head had battered off almost every step.

He stopped, three stairs from the bottom. "Why isn't there blood?"

Mel carried on past him. "He might be OK. Maybe he just needs—"

"Mel, wait!" Drake cried, pulling her back just in time. With a mechanical *whirr*, Bingo's legs and arms twisted backwards, raising his chest up towards the ceiling. His head spun all the way round until his face was pointed towards the floor. He looked like a dog wearing a human-suit, but the truth was,

Drake knew, that he was neither of those things.

"OK," Mel gasped, stepping back. She glanced sideways at Drake. "Explain this one. Now."

"He's a robot," Drake told her.

"A *robot*?"

"In the cupboard. Dr Black must've done something to the real one and let the robot take his place."

Mel frowned. "But wouldn't that mean...?"

They both turned to look at the other two bullies. Circles of red light flickered on in the dark centres of Dim and Spud's eyes.

Down on the floor, Bingo's mouth pulled into an electric snarl. "Kill them," he commanded. "Kill them both!"

"Move!" Drake yelped. Catching Mel by the arm he jumped the final few steps. Using Bingo's chest as a springboard, they raced along the corridor towards the fire exit.

Dim and Spud bent over and wrapped their hands round their own ankles. The lines of their backs curved to form two almost perfect circles and they rolled, like hula hoops, down the stairs.

Drake pushed down the bar of the fire exit and the door swung wide. A piercing alarm began to scream, drawing the attention of the hundred or so kids dotted around the concrete rectangle before them.

"Get out of the way!" Drake bellowed, as he and Mel spilled out of the school. "Move, it's not safe, it's not—"

A crashing sound drowned him out. The spinning circles that were Spud and Dim punched through the walls on either side of the door, spraying chunks of stone and slivers of glass. The school grounds were filled with the sound of screaming as Spud and Dim pursued Drake and Mel across the concrete.

Drake sprinted on, pushing his way through the panicked masses, pulling Mel behind him. The robots were too fast. There was no way he could outrun them. He had to dodge round the crowds, but Dim and Spud ploughed through them, scattering schoolkids like skittles.

Frantically, Drake shoved two fingers in his mouth and blew. Air hissed out like a slow puncture. The spinning hoops were almost upon them now. "Come on," Drake pleaded. "Just *whistle!*"

He blew again. There was no sound, but suddenly a horse was there, rearing up in front of them, sending the school yard into even greater chaos.

Fluid dripped from the white horse's mouth, and from

its eyes, and from the weeping sores that covered its flanks. Pestilence slid down from the saddle, and pulled Drake and Mel in behind him. Then he faced the rapidly approaching bullies, and did the last thing Drake would have expected.

He took off his rubber gloves.

The two bullies spun to a stop and straightened up in front of him. Pest held his hands up, palms facing them.

"Tell me, gents, do you know what 'Guinea Worm Disease' is?" he asked.

Dim and Spud didn't reply.

"It's a rather unfortunate medical condition that results in a metre-long worm growing inside your stomach, then chewing its way out through the nearest available exit. It's not contagious." Pestilence looked at both of his hands in turn. "Usually."

Drake tapped him on the shoulder. "Uh, Pest..."

"One second, Drake," Pestilence said. "I was just about to share something with your *friends* here."

"But, Pest, you don't—"

"Leave this to me, Drake. I *do* know what I'm doing."

He pressed his hands against the bullies' foreheads. A sickly green glow spread out from his palm and fingertips. Dim and

Spud stared at him, their faces impassive. Pestilence's delicate features creased into a frown.

"That's what I was trying to tell you," Drake said. "Techno-magic mumbo jumbo. They're robots."

Pestilence's face went several shades paler. "Robots? Ah, so is that how they did the spinny thing? I did wonder." He withdrew his hands. "Wasting my time with that, then," he said. He smiled nervously. "We should probably go."

"One step ahead of you, Uncle Bob," Mel said. She was sitting on the horse, towards the back of the saddle. Pest leaped up in front of her, and they both pulled Drake up between them.

"Hold on," Pest warned. Drake felt Mel's hands on his waist. They gripped him tightly as she pulled herself close against his back.

Pestilence flicked the reins, and the world around them became a streak of speed.

"Hey, Chief," Mel said into Drake's ear.

"Yeah?"

She tightened her grip round his waist. "Your family is frickin' *nuts*."

CHAPTER TWENTY-SIX

THE HORSE RACED through a row of back gardens, leaping the hedges and fences between them with practised ease. Despite the animal's performance, though, Mel was concerned.

"I think your horse needs a vet," she said, as they all ducked under a washing line. "He's bleeding out of, well, everywhere."

"Yeah, he does that," Drake told her. "He's fine, though."

"Fit as a fiddle," Pestilence chimed.

"My, uh, predecessor," Drake said, keeping his voice low. "I found out who he is. His name's Dr Black, he's a teacher at my school."

"Really? Interesting. But not our biggest worry at the minute."

"What? Why? What's happening?" Drake asked.

They'd left the robo-bullies back near the school. Dim and Spud had spun after them for a few hundred metres, but the horse had easily outpaced them. Even so, Drake shuddered to think what they and Dr Black might be up to now.

"We're taking Mel home," Pest said. He leaned round in the saddle. "I like what you've done with your hair, by the way."

"Thanks," Mel said. "But I don't want to go home. I want someone to tell me what's going on."

"The end of the world," said Pest. He turned and met Drake's eye. "We've had the call."

"What call?" asked Mel.

"*The* call?" Drake gasped.

"*What* call? Will someone please tell me what's happening?"

The horse stopped, suddenly and without warning. Drake looked along a gravel driveway at a large house with two cars parked out front.

He swung down, just a little awkwardly. Mel dismounted beside him. She stared at him expectantly. "Well?"

"Look, the thing is," Drake said. "I'm not really entirely sure what's going on myself, so I don't know how to explain any of it."

"Try."

Drake's mouth moved, as if testing out the words before he said them. "The Horsemen of the Apocalypse live in my garden," he said. "No, wait, that makes me sound mental."

"It does a bit," Mel agreed.

Drake tried to think of another way of phrasing it. "No," he realised, "that's pretty much it. The Horsemen of the Apocalypse live in my garden. Or three of them do, anyway. Dr Black used to be the fourth. He was Death, but he got bored of waiting for the Apocalypse, so he left to destroy the world on his own. And so I'm the new one."

"You're the new Death?" Mel said.

Drake smiled faintly. "Pretty hard to believe, right?"

"So, who's he?" she asked, jabbing a thumb at the man on horseback beside them.

"Pestilence," Drake said. "He's not really my Uncle Bob. I made that up."

Mel nodded. "I didn't think he looked like a Bob."

"*Thank* you! See? I thought maybe Alejandro or—"

"Not now, Pest."

Mel looked at the two of them, then at the horse. "So, what happens now?" she asked.

Drake's eyes widened. "What, you mean you believe me?"

"I just saw a cat change into a... thing that wasn't a cat," Mel said. "And some kids I've known for ten years become killer robot hula-hoops. Right now, I'll believe pretty much anything you tell me."

Drake found himself smiling. Mel didn't join in.

"So, it's happening?" she asked. "He's really going to destroy the world, like you said?"

Drake nodded. "It looks like it."

"We need to move," said Pestilence softly. "The others will be waiting."

"Uh, yeah," Drake mumbled. "Just a minute."

"We made a deal, remember?" Mel said. "This morning. We made a deal. I thought you were kidding, but... we made a deal. If he's trying to destroy the world, we stop him, remember?"

He nodded. "I remember."

"OK, then. Good," she said. She leaned in and kissed him, just briefly, on the lips.

"What was that for?" he asked, when she pulled away.

"Luck," Mel said. "Something tells me you're going to need it."

✦

The shed looked different when Drake and Pest stepped inside. It took Drake a moment to realise why. The square table at which the horsemen usually sat had been pushed off to one side. Three of the chairs were stacked neatly on top of it. Famine's reinforced seat was half tucked underneath.

"High time you got here," said War as they both entered. He bent down and caught hold of a circle of metal that was set into the floor. Had the table still been there, the handle would have been almost completely concealed.

War pulled and a wide hatch swung upwards, revealing a stairway leading down into a brightly lit chamber beneath the shed. "Famine's already down there," he said. "Getting ready."

"Getting ready?" said Drake. "What do you mean, getting ready?"

"Well, he's hardly going to usher in the Apocalypse in a baggy grey tracksuit, is he?" War said. "He's getting into uniform, like we all should've done ten minutes ago."

"No, but listen, it's not the real Apocalypse," Drake said. "It's Dr Black, the old Death, he's the one doing it."

War blinked. "So?"

"*So?* What do you mean, *so?* So it's not the real Apocalypse."

"Who's to say what is and isn't the Apocalypse? For all we know, this was always how it was going to end." He gestured with his head for Drake to go down the steps. "Now come on. Shift it."

It wasn't a single room beneath the shed, as Drake had been expecting. It was a complex. The walls were painted in clinical white, and a dozen corridors led off in a dozen different directions. There were four doors set into the walls, each a different colour. One was white, one was red, one was black and the final one was a pale, sickly green. Black and white squares of vinyl covered the floor, and row after row of fluorescent lights buzzed softly overhead.

In the centre of this room were four leather couches, laid out in a square. A glass coffee table sat between them, with magazines stacked neatly on top. It looked like the waiting room of an expensive dentist.

Pestilence, then War, joined him at the foot of the steps. "What is this place?" Drake asked.

"It's a... shared area, between the afterlives. We rent some space from the management company," War said dismissively.

He turned to Pest. "Go get ready."

"Righty-ho," Pestilence said. He smiled, but it sat uneasily on him. "See you soon, then."

War caught Drake by the scruff of the neck. "You, with me," he said, marching him towards the red door.

They pushed through into a locker room, with wooden benches lining three of the walls. There were just two lockers. They stood back to back in the centre of the room.

"That's yours, that's mine," said War, indicating which was which.

"How come we're not all here?" Drake asked.

"We've all got our own changing rooms," War explained. "I moved your locker in here so we could have a little chat about what happens next."

"What does happen next?"

"Get dressed," War said. He opened his locker and pulled out a gleaming breastplate.

Almost in a trance, Drake opened his locker. The Robe of Sorrows was hung up inside. He unhooked it and lifted it out. The material felt like damp velvet beneath his fingers.

"Do I put it on?" he asked. His voice wobbled. His heart thudded in his chest. He didn't want to be going along with any of this, but every time he thought about resisting, the notion quickly slipped away.

"What do you think?" War snapped. He was wearing the breastplate over his usual leather armour now, and was pulling on a pair of thick leather gauntlets.

Drake's arms, moving almost entirely of their own accord, slipped the Robe of Sorrows over his head.

"It's too big," he said.

A shiver ran down his spine as the black folds oozed and writhed across his skin. In moments, the robe was a perfect fit.

"Oh," he said. "No, it isn't."

"Keep the hood down for now," War told him. "No point putting it up until the big moment."

Drake nodded. He didn't want to put the hood up. He didn't want to wear the thing at all. "You didn't answer my question," he said. "What happens next?"

War closed his locker door with a *clang*. His breastplate gleamed. His leather gauntlets *creaked* as he flexed his fingers in and out. "I don't know," he said. "You tell me."

"What? How should I know?"

"You said he was someone from your school. Did he tell

you anything? Like what he was planning?"

"No," Drake said. "Just that it was going to be something spectacular."

"Aye, that sounds like him," War said. "Bloody show-off. Anything else?"

"Not really. He had a smartphone thing. He pushed a button and said that was that, he'd started it all happening. Then Toxie appeared and attacked him."

War slid his sword into the scabbard on his back. "Oh. So he's dead?"

"He fought back," Drake told him.

"Fought back? Against Toxie? Against a Hellhound?"

"Yeah," Drake said with a shrug. "Seemed to be putting up a pretty good fight too."

"What did you say his name was, this teacher?"

"Dr Black."

War pulled a face that said the name meant nothing to him. "New, is he?"

"No, been there a while, I think."

"Really? Interesting," War said, stroking his beard. "Right, get the Deathblade and we'll go and meet the others."

"Where is it?" Drake asked.

"It's there, in the locker."

Drake looked inside the empty locker. "No, it isn't."

War was suddenly behind him. "It was there," he growled. "I know it was there."

"Well, it's not there now," Drake said.

War muttered something below his breath. "Doesn't matter," he said aloud. "We'll make do without it. Let's go and get the other two."

Drake wanted to say 'no'. He wanted to argue with the horseman, to convince him to call the whole thing off, but it was as if he were hypnotised. So, while he wanted to say 'no', what he actually said was: 'OK.'

They left the locker room, then stopped abruptly when they saw the other two horsemen waiting for them.

"Ta-daa!" chimed Pestilence, holding out his arms. "What do you think?"

A stunned silence fell.

Pestilence looked like a violent encounter between a motorcyclist and a cowboy. On his bottom half he wore black leather chaps over his usual white trousers. Tassels dangled along the seams, swishing outwards when he turned to give the other horsemen a twirl.

His boots, which reached almost to his knees, were also leather, but shinier than the chaps. They finished with a large, square heel at the back, giving Pest another few centimetres in height.

The leather jacket he wore was studded across the shoulders. It hung open, revealing a black waistcoat underneath and, below that, a white roll-neck sweater.

There was a soft *creak* as Pestilence pulled on his cap. Also leather. Also studded, with a chain hanging across the front, just above the peak.

War, at last, found his voice.

"What... in the name of God... are you wearing?"

Pest looked down at his outfit. "What's the matter with it?"

"That's your official uniform, is it?" asked War, in the tones of someone who was a hair's breadth away from the end of his tether.

"More or less," Pest said. "I just sort of... zooshed it up a bit. It's leather. Very practical, leather."

War shook his head, then turned to Famine. He was still wearing the same faded grey tracksuit as before. "And what's your story?" War asked.

"It doesn't fit," Famine said. "I can't get the trousers past my knees. I ripped the backside right out of them trying to pull them on."

"And what about the measuring scales? You're supposed to appear carrying scales. It says so in the book."

Famine looked uncomfortable. "Yeah, I sort of sat on them."

War's forehead twitched. "You mean you broke them?"

"Not exactly, not exactly," Famine said. "See, I was trying to pull the trousers on at the time, and I didn't know the scales were on the seat, and, well..." His voice trailed off and he gave a wobbly shrug. "I could try to get them back, I suppose, but I might need a hand. And some sort of lubricant."

Pest's face went an interesting shade of green. "I think I'm going to be sick."

"Great," War growled, looking up to the ceiling. "Just great. You've lost your scythe, you've wedged your scales where the sun doesn't shine and you..." he looked Pest up and down. "I don't know where to start. Some bloody Apocalypse this is going to be."

"Speaking of which, we'd best get a move on," Pest said. He took a deep breath, then turned to Drake and positioned his mouth into something that wasn't quite a smile, but was a good effort all the same. "You ready, then?"

Drake felt himself nod. The weight of thousands of years of expectation pushed down on him, smothering his will to resist. He was Death, the fourth Horseman of the Apocalypse, and he had a job to do.

"Said your goodbyes to everyone?" pressed Pest. "You know, to your mum, and all that?"

"My mum?" Drake mumbled, as if confused by the word. Then his eyes went wide and his head went light, and like that, the spell was broken. "My mum! My mum's going to die. *Everyone* is going to die!"

Drake's breath came in big, shaky gulps, too fast for his lungs to cope with. "We can't do this. We can't go through with it. We can't."

War shot Pestilence an angry glare. "Oh, well done. Nice work." He gestured with a thumb towards the hatch. "Get upstairs, the pair of you. We'll be up in a minute."

"But... the Apocalypse," Pest said. "What if we're late? We can't be late!"

"What are they gonnae do? Fire us?"

"No, but they could banish us to Hell," Famine said.

"Aye, just let me see them try it," War snapped. "Now get upstairs. We'll be up in a bit."

Famine and Pest exchanged a worried look, but they both knew better than to argue with War. Drake watched them until they had clumped all the way up the stairs, and out through the hatch at the top. Only then did he turn to the other horseman.

"We've got to do something," Drake said. "We can't let this happen. All the people, we can't just let them die."

"Sit down," War told him. A leather couch squeaked in surprise as War's full weight came down on it.

"What?" Drake spluttered. "There's no time!"

"Sit down and catch your breath," War insisted. He lifted a magazine, then rested his enormous feet on the coffee table. "You're nervous. I get it. Take a minute to get your head together."

"My head is together. I'm not nervous," Drake said. "That's nothing to do with it. It's just... it's wrong. It's all wrong!"

"Aye. It's hardly surprising, you seeing it that way. You've only been in the job a day. No wonder it's messing with your head."

There was something different about War's voice. It

took Drake several seconds to realise what it was. He wasn't shouting. "I'm gonnae let you in on a wee secret," War said.

Despite himself, Drake took a step closer. "What?"

War held up the magazine. There was a salmon on the cover. "I always wanted to go fishing," he said.

Drake blinked. "What?" he asked, for a second time.

"Fishing. I always wanted to go, but never did. Don't know why, really." He flicked through a few pages. "You ever fished?"

"No, I... Why are you telling me this?"

"I'd have liked a boat too," War continued. "You know where you are with a boat."

"On the water, usually," Drake said automatically.

"Exactly." War sighed and sat the magazine down. "Still, too late now, I suppose. Missed out on that opportunity." He looked over at a clock on the wall, then picked up another magazine. It was a thin, glossy one, filled with 'Real Life' stories sent in by readers.

War scanned the cover, picking out the headlines. "*My baby breathes through his ears,*" he read. "Look at this one. *Cannibals ate my feet.*"

"What? So what? What are you on about?"

"It's life's rich tapestry," War said. "Check this one. *I'm afraid of my own hair.* Her own hair. The nutter." He turned a page and chuckled at another headline. "They're a strange old bunch, humans. Interesting. Annoying, a lot of the time, aye, but... interesting."

Drake watched the giant, as he casually flipped through the magazine, occasionally chuckling at some story or other. He didn't know why, but as he looked down at War, a question just popped in there, right at the front of Drake's thoughts.

"Do you want to do it?"

War's eyes lifted and glared over the top of the magazine. "What?"

"I asked if you wanted it to happen. Do you want the Apocalypse?"

"Do I want it? What do you mean, do I want it? What are you saying?"

"You don't, do you?" Drake realised. Excitement flushed through him. "It doesn't have to happen. Don't you see? We can stop it."

"Stop it?" roared War, suddenly back on his feet and looming larger than he had ever loomed before. "*Stop it?*

Have you even read your job description?"

"You didn't give me a job description," replied Drake, standing his ground.

"Well, it's the exact opposite of what you just said," War barked. "We don't stop Armageddon, we welcome it in."

Drake searched his face. "But you don't want to."

"What I want has nothing to do with it!" War bellowed.

"Just admit it," Drake shouted back. "Say it."

The bit of War's face that wasn't beard turned scarlet. "Admit what? That I don't want the Apocalypse to happen now because I'm worried you'll mess it up? That I don't want to have wasted six-and-a-half thousand years waiting for the end of the world, only for you to come along and ruin it for everyone?"

War kicked one of the couches so hard it flipped across the room and thudded against a wall. "You are without doubt the *worst* Death we've ever had," he boomed. "And I'm including the goldfish in that. You're not picking any of it up, you haven't developed any of the abilities, you can't even whistle! We'll be a laughing stock!"

The gleaming breastplate rose and fell as War took a series of deep, steadying breaths. "So, in answer to your question, no I don't want the world to end. At least, not today," he admitted.

"Besides," he added more quietly, "I'd quite like to try fishing."

"Well, OK, then," said Drake. "So what are we going to do about it?"

"What's taking them so long?" sighed Pestilence. He was wearing a hole in the floor, pacing back and forth, his eyes trained on the open hatch. "It's all very well War taking his time, he's not the first horseman. I am. If we turn up late, who do you think's going to get the blame? Muggins here, that's who."

There was a sound of footsteps from below. Drake hurried up the steps and into the shed, with War at his heels.

"Finally!" Pest said. He gave Drake a friendly smile, then looked to War. "Is that us ready for the off, then? Judgement Day's not going to start itself!"

"Aye, about that," said War, with a sideways glance at Drake. "There's been a bit of a change of plan."

CHAPTER TWENTY-SEVEN

THE FOUR HORSEMEN of the Apocalypse stood in the clearing outside the shed. They were arguing. Or rather, three of them were arguing. The other was having a Cornetto.

"Have you lost your minds?" Pestilence asked, looking from War to Drake and back again. "I mean, I mean... The entire point of our existence is to usher in the end of the world. *Usher it in*, not put a stop to it. Have you lost your minds?"

"We don't know if this *is* the end of the world, though, do we?" Drake said. "It's the old Death doing it, so it's probably not the real thing."

"Of course it is! War got the call!"

"Aye, but they've lost the book," War said.

"That was careless," Famine said, taking a bite from his cone.

Pestilence's gloved hands went to his mouth. "They've lost the book? The Book of Everything? They can't have lost the Book of Everything. How could they lose the Book of Everything?"

War shrugged. "No idea, but they have. They don't know anything for sure. It's guesswork. They told me on the phone earlier, but I didn't want to say anything, in case, you know, you had a breakdown or something. But aye, they've lost the book."

"Oh, well... It doesn't matter," Pest said, after some consideration. "We got the call. It's not our job to question, it's our job to ride across the sky. Come on, War, we've been waiting a long time for this. We can't blow it now."

"But that's exactly what *will* happen if we ride out with him in tow," War stabbed a finger at Drake. "He can't even summon his horse."

"The end can't come soon enough for my liking," said Famine. "All this sitting around's doing my head in."

"We don't have to sit around all the time, though," Drake said. "There's a world of things to do out there – you don't have to sit in a shed playing board games. You could go fishing, or hillwalking, or take up, I don't know, showjumping or something." Drake aimed the next suggestion squarely at Famine. "You could get a job reviewing restaurants, or, God, I don't know, join a theatre group."

Pestilence briefly raised both eyebrows. "Musical theatre?"

"If you wanted," Drake said, nodding enthusiastically. "You were created at the beginning of the world, and you've been waiting around for the end. But you've missed out on the middle bit in between. You've wasted it."

Famine and Pest exchanged a look. Behind his beard, War smiled.

"It's too late," Pestilence said, but he didn't sound sure of himself. "We've had the call."

"OK, then what if this is the end of the world?" Drake asked. "What if this is the big finale? What happens to us afterwards?"

"Well, I mean we..." Pestilence began, but he stopped there. He looked to War. "What happens to us again?"

War's broad shoulders raised, then lowered. "Dunno. You got your contract?"

"I lost it years ago," Pestilence said. He tried to smile, but his face was having none of it. "I expect we just... what? Go to Heaven? I expect that's it."

Famine crammed the last of the Cornetto into his mouth. "Hang on," he mumbled, before swallowing. "Lemme check the old filing system."

The fat man cleared his throat noisily. He sucked in his belly, but it was hard to notice any difference. He cleared his throat again, then punched a fist against the top of his stomach, right below where it met his chest bone.

"You might want to step away," War said, guiding Drake a few paces back. Pestilence was looking the other way, his rubber-gloved hands over his ears, his eyes tightly closed.

There was a sound like a cat vomiting up a furball. Famine's face was turning a moody shade of purple as he struck himself again and again below the sternum.

"Uh, should we help him?" Drake asked.

War shook his head. "I wouldn't recommend it."

With a final spluttering cough, Famine hacked up a tight roll of paper, wrapped in a clear plastic cover. It landed with a soggy *splat* on the ground.

"Told you," War said.

Groaning with the effort, Famine stooped and retrieved

the package. He wiped it on his tracksuit to dry it, then removed the waterproof wrapper and uncurled his contract of employment.

"Is it over?" Pest asked, opening one eye. When he saw that Famine was no longer regurgitating paperwork, he opened the other eye and brought both hands down from his ears.

Famine's sausage-fingers fumbled slowly through the pages. Somewhere near the last page, he stopped. His bloated lips moved silently as he read.

"Anything?" War asked.

Famine nodded. "We become human, apparently."

Pestilence's lips seemed to tighten. "What? When?"

War snatched the contract from Famine and skimmed over the page. "Right away," he said, at last. "Soon as we've finished riding." He passed the contract back to Famine. "You know what that means?"

"We'll be judged," Pest gasped. "With the rest of them. We'll all be judged."

"Still reckon we should go through with it?" War asked him.

Pest's face had gone pale. Paler, even, than usual. "We have to," he whimpered. "Don't we?"

"The way I see it," said War, "is that, one, we don't know if this is the real Apocalypse..."

"If it *was* the real one there would be signs," Drake said, remembering the conversation on Pest's horse. "You said so yourself. Raining blood, plagues of locusts, all that. You seen any locusts around here lately?"

"No," Pestilence admitted. He wrung his hands together, nervously. "But, still—"

"*Two*," said War, irritated by the interruption, "if it is the real Apocalypse, then this clown is only going to make a right mess of it. No offence."

"None taken," Drake assured him.

"Three, we'll be judged along with the humans, which I don't fancy one little bit."

Pest chewed his lip. "I know all that, but... it's our job. We've got to go through with it."

War squeezed the bridge of his nose between two gloved fingers. He sighed loudly, then looked Pest squarely in the eye.

"I'm only going to say this once," he said, his voice low. "And after that, we're never going to talk about it again." He cleared his throat. "I... don't mind being in the shed with you both. I complain about it, aye, and half the time you do my head right in, with your whingeing and moaning and arguing and—"

"Was there a point coming?" asked Drake.

"What? Oh, aye. Aye." War looked up to the sky, then back at Pest and Famine. "If I'm being honest, the other reasons don't matter. The fact of it is, I don't want the Apocalypse. I thought I did, but I don't. I don't want everything to end. I don't want us three to end."

"Us four," said Pest, nodding in Drake's direction.

"Aye. Well. Whatever. I'm just... I'm not ready for it. Not yet."

Pest looked across the faces of the others. "What'll happen if we don't ride?"

War shrugged. "No idea."

An anxious smile twitched across Pestilence's lips. "Well, then I guess we'll find out," he said. He saw the surprise in War's eyes. "It's Wednesday, isn't it? I mean, come on. Who has Armageddon on a Wednesday?"

"So, we put a stop to it," Drake said. There was a commanding tone in his voice that even he hadn't heard before. "Agreed?"

"Agreed," said War.

"OK," said Pest, not quite so confidently.

They turned to look at Famine. He had re-wrapped his contract and now had his head back as he crammed the roll of paper down his throat. There was a series of short *ack-ack-ack* sounds, before he swallowed it down.

"Sorry, wasn't listening," he admitted. "What's happening?"

"We're stopping the end of the world," Drake told him.

"We can't do that!" Famine protested. "We got the call, so we have to—"

"There'll be a cake in it for you," War told him.

Famine's face became deathly serious. "I'm in. What's the plan?"

"Dr Black's probably still at the school," Drake said. "If we can find out what he did maybe we can figure out how to reverse it."

"Right then, gents," War intoned. "Time to summon our rides. Stick to the ground, though. No going airborne."

"We'd get there quicker if we did," Famine said.

"Aye, but we don't want to kick Armageddon into top gear accidentally by riding across the sky, do we?" War said. "We stick to the ground."

"Good call," said Pest, stepping forward. He thrust a gloved hand into the inside pocket of his suit. "But before we go anywhere..." He pulled out four matching badges. "If we're going to do this, let's do it properly."

Drake took the one with 'I AM 4' printed on it and balanced it in his palm. It was heavier than it looked, about the weight of a pound coin. He opened the fastener and tried to attach the badge to his robe, but the pin would not go through the thick material.

He tried to force the pin through, but the material refused to give. "What's this made of?" he asked, pushing the pin so hard it bent double.

"Solidified darkness," War said.

"Oh, right," Drake said, who by this point had stopped being surprised by anything the horsemen told him. He looked up and saw that they were wearing their badges. Even War had found somewhere on his armour to attach the thing. Pest stared at him expectantly.

"Um, the robe bent it," he explained. "I'll stick it in the pocket."

Pestilence gave a sigh. "I don't know. You try to do something nice..."

"Right," said War, interrupting him, "let's do this."

Pheeeeeep!

Pest's whistle was short and shrill. Even before the sound had faded, a sonic boom raced around the garden.

"'And I heard, as it were, the noise of thunder'," quoted War, as the white horse tore through a hole in space and landed with a thudding of hooves on the grass.

War himself whistled next, and there came his red horse, leaping from nowhere, its mane spluttering like fire as it clip-clopped to a stop beside them.

Famine stuck two fingers in his mouth. The sound came out accompanied by a spray of saliva, but it was still unmistakeably a whistle.

No horse appeared. Drake stood, watching on expectantly, waiting for the thunder of hooves. He was just about to suggest that Famine try again, when he did hear something. It was a low whine, not unlike the sound of the air conditioning in Dr Black's cupboard, and back in the cave.

A ripple appeared in the air half a dozen or so metres ahead of them. A black shape lurched through, trundling along on its four hard-rubber wheels. The electric engine rose in pitch as the vehicle passed them, before returning to a low hum when it stopped by the horses.

"Mobility scooter," Famine explained. He smiled shyly. "Like I said, haven't ridden in a while."

"Your turn," War said, turning to Drake.

Drake shook his head. "I... I don't think I can."

"You can do it," Pest said encouragingly. "We believe in you!"

Drake glanced between them all, then gave a single determined nod. "I can do this," he said. He curled his thumb and index finger, stuck them in his mouth and blew.

Pffffff.

He blew again, harder this time.

Pffffflllffff.

"Oh, forget it," said War. He was already on his horse. In one moved he hoisted Drake off his feet and deposited him on the saddle behind him. "Seriously," he told him. "Worst Death *ever*."

"Don't you listen to him," said Pest, settling himself into his saddle. "Oh, so you can't whistle. So what?" He smiled and winked. "It's hardly the end of the world."

The horses clattered towards the school gates, scattering the crowds that had gathered there. Hundreds of children in matching school uniform lined the fence, held back by men and women in an altogether different type of uniform.

Yellow 'Do Not Cross' tape had been draped across the gate. Beyond it, more uniformed officers stood, their eyes trained on a window mid-way along the first floor.

"Police," Drake said. "How are we going to get past them?"

War flicked the reins and his horse sped up. A clattering at their back told them that Pest too had picked up the pace. Several hundred metres behind them, Famine twisted the throttle of his mobility scooter, but it was already going at top speed and had nothing more to give.

With a "Yah!" from War, the horse leaped over the metal fence. Drake heard the gasp from the people below as the animal sailed over their heads. Sparks sprayed into the air as its hooves skidded down on to the school grounds.

Another gasp; another spark shower, and Pestilence's horse touched down beside them. The police were racing over as the three horsemen dismounted.

"Oi, who the Hell are you? What do you think you're doing?"

War didn't bother to look at them. "Pest," he said, waving a hand vaguely.

Pestilence gave a gentle cough, then opened his mouth wide. There was a sound like rushing air and a faint green haze wafted from within his throat. The first row of police officers toppled backwards as the cloud hit them. The next row froze in confusion, and then they too were falling.

The rest of the police pushed back, even as the crowd began to panic. Their reaction had come too late, though. The green mist rolled across them, filling their airways even as they started to scream.

Like dominoes they fell, those closest to the school first, then the row behind, then the row behind that one. It took just seconds until the only movement beyond the school gates was the steady flashing of the police car lights.

"Did... did you kill them?" Drake asked.

"What do you take me for?" said Pest, slapping him on the upper arm. "Temporary narcolepsy. They're all just having a bit of a nap. Be right as rain in twenty minutes."

"Then we'd better move fast," War said. He pointed up to the window the police had been so fixated on. "Is that the classroom?"

"Uh, yeah. I think so," Drake said. "Looks about right. Should we wait for Famine?"

"He'll only slow us down," said War. He was already unsheathing his immense sword as he strode towards the door. "It's up to the three of us. Let's go and get this over with."

CHAPTER TWENTY-EIGHT

THE WOODEN DOUBLE-DOORS at the front entrance to the school were closed over when they approached. Drake turned the metal ring handles and the doors swung outwards, revealing a solid metal barrier behind them.

Drake rapped his knuckles against the metal. They made a sound like the chiming of some ancient bell. "He's sealed himself in," Drake realised. He set off running. "There's a hole round the side," he said, racing towards the spot where Dim and Spud had torn through the wall.

He stopped, mid-way across the school yard. A wall of shiny chrome covered the hole like a sticking-plaster. "We can't get in," Drake cried. "He's blocked us out."

"You know your problem? Well, one of them, anyway?" War growled. "You give up far too easily."

The giant hurled his sword. It flipped, end over end, before the blade buried itself in the rectangle of metal. Gripping the hilt with both hands, War dragged the blade across, then down. He pulled the sword free, then fired a kick against the damaged metal. It *squealed*, then swung inwards.

"Nae bother," he said, ducking his head as he led the other two horsemen into the school.

"Up here," Drake told them. He took the stairs two at a time until he reached the top. In moments, he was outside Dr Black's classroom. He didn't even wait for the others to catch up before pushing into the room.

The first thing he saw was Toxie. The cat-faced Hellhound was on his side, half buried by broken furniture. His chest rose and fell in shallow breaths, and a puddle of dark, almost purple blood pooled on the floor around him.

"I figured, if I killed him, he'd only come back."

Drake spun to find Dr Black sitting behind his desk. His clothes were torn and scorched in places, but otherwise he seemed none the worse for his battle with Toxie.

"So I let him live. But only just."

"You *monster*!"

Drake hadn't even heard the other horsemen enter the

room, but Pestilence's voice was suddenly there in his ear.

"Yes," Dr Black chuckled. "I know. So good to see you again, Pest."

"Yeah?" Pest sniffed. "Well... well... not likewise."

"Still as devastatingly witty as ever, I see," Dr Black noted.

"We've come to stop you," Drake told him. "To stop... whatever it is you're doing."

The teacher blinked, then threw back his head and laughed. "Stop me?" he said. "Didn't they explain to you how this whole thing is supposed to work? This is the end, boy. This is the *Apocalypse*. That word mean anything to you? You can't stop me. No one can stop me."

War took a step closer, his hand tightening round his sword. "Remember me?"

"Ah, War. I advise you to stay where you are," Dr Black warned. He was on his feet, suddenly serious. "You know why all those police are out there? You know why the crowd has gathered?"

He beckoned with his finger for them to follow, as he made his way to the cupboard. "Because I have hostages," he said, in a sing-song voice. With a kick, he opened the door to reveal Mel sitting on the floor beside Mr Franks. The young teacher was awake, but still flat on his back.

"Drake?" Mel cried, before the door was pulled closed again.

"She came back to check on him. Isn't that noble?" Dr Black asked. His face was lit up with a manic glee as he strolled over and leaned an elbow on the windowsill. "But now I have them both."

"In the cupboard," War said.

"Precisely!"

"But you're not in the cupboard. And neither are we." With two big paces, War positioned himself directly in front of the cupboard door. "And now you can't *get* in the cupboard, either."

Dr Black's grin remained fixed, but his eyes had begun darting left and right, as if War's meaning was very slowly becoming clear.

"So, what he's saying," Pest explained, "is that you have now effectively lost your hostages."

"And we're free to kick your ass," Drake concluded. He pointed to the bearded giant on his left. "Well, mostly him."

Dr Black's smile had gone completely now. "There's only one little problem," he said.

"What's that?" asked Drake.

"You're going to have to catch me first!"

With a *crash*, the teacher hurled himself through the window behind him. The horsemen raced over in time to see him crunch face-first on to the concrete twenty metres below.

"Ooh, that's going to hurt," Pest winced. Even before the sentence was out of his mouth, though, Dr Black had begun to move. He got quickly to his feet, looked up at the window, and smiled.

"That's not right," War frowned. "He shouldn't be able to do that."

Dr Black was off and running, racing towards the two steeds standing together by the school gates.

"The horses," Pest gasped. "He's going for the horses."

"Bugger that," War growled. "After him!"

With a twitch of his legs, War propelled himself through the window, taking a large chunk of wall out with him. Drake leaned over and watched as War landed on his feet, then began to sprint across the school grounds after Dr Black.

"Ready?" asked Pest, taking a series of quick, deep breaths.

"For what?" Drake asked. "We're not... We can't jump that!"

"Yes, we can. We're the Horsemen of the Apocalypse. We can do lots of things," Pest said. A rubber-gloved hand caught Drake by the sleeve and pulled him towards the hole.

Drake screamed as gravity took hold. The wind whipped around him and he felt Pest's grip slip from his arm. His limbs flailed wildly. The wind continued to whip around him. He screamed some more. Flailing. Wind. Screaming.

He had just begun to think it was taking a very long time for him to hit the ground, when he hit the ground. His knees crunched on to the concrete first, then his shoulder, then the top of his head as his momentum bounced him over on to his back. He lay there, quite still, looking up at the broken window and idly wondering if he were still alive.

"See?" said Pest, leaning over him. "That wasn't so bad, was it?"

Dr Black raced across the school yard, moving faster than any human being had any right to. Each bound covered well over a metre, like a triple jumper preparing for take-off, but never quite reaching that final spectacular leap.

Had any of the gathered crowds been awake to watch him, they'd have thought he was running impossibly fast.

But they would also have thought that the bearded man behind him was running faster. And they would have been right.

Dr Black glanced over his shoulder, realised he wasn't going to have time to get on a horse, and so carried on past them. He tore through the yellow police tape and went rushing out on to the street beyond.

There, surrounded by the unconscious forms of his former pupils, he stopped, turned and waited for the coming of War.

"Given up, have you?" War boomed, slowing to a jog, then finally, to a stop. "Realised you can't escape?"

"I wasn't trying to escape, you idiot," Dr Black told him, as Drake and Pestilence ran up to join them. "I was drawing you away."

"What?" Drake asked. "What are you talking about?" He glanced nervously at War. "What's he talking about?"

"It's not him," War said. "He was never Death."

Dr Black's eyes lit up. *Literally* lit up. "Can you say *decoy*?" he grinned. He was still grinning as War brought his sword slicing down towards his head.

There was the sound of metal slicing metal, and the tip of War's blade buried itself in the concrete at his feet. Something gave a faint *fizzle*, and sparks began to flicker along the thin line that now ran the length of Dr Black's body.

"You can't stop him, you know," the robot informed them, even as both halves of it began to fall in opposite directions. "The world ends today, and there's nothing you can do to—"

The halves hit the ground. The voice faded and the glow in the android's eyes grew dark. War yanked his sword free of the tarmac, then poked one half of Dr Black with his toe. "Techno-magic mumbo jumbo," he said.

"What...? But...? How did you know?" Drake asked. "It was him. I was sure it was him!"

"I had my doubts, but I couldn't say for sure until I'd seen him with my own two eyes. He fought a Hellhound, then face-planted twenty metres on to concrete without winding up a messy splat. Death Nine's human now, and no human could do that. Besides, you said yourself, he'd been there for ages," War shrugged. "He couldn't be Death. Death's barely been human a few weeks. He would have to be someone new."

An icy needle of shock pricked at the centre of Drake's chest. "New?"

"Aye. Stands to reason."

It hit Drake like a sledgehammer. He reached for the fence to support himself, but his hand slipped and he lurched to one side. "Mr Franks," he said in a barely audible whisper.

"Who?"

"Mr Franks. *Darren Franks*. D.F."

"What you on about?"

"The other teacher. The one in the cupboard. *He's* the old Death, and we've left him with Mel!"

"Helloooo!" called a voice from nearby. Famine was slowly approaching on his scooter, waving enthusiastically with one hand, while frantically trying to steer with the other. "Be with you in a minute."

Drake didn't wait for Famine, and he didn't wait for the other horsemen. He ran back towards the school gates, his pounding heart making his legs move faster than they had ever moved before, until...

PZZZZKT!

A shock of pure agony exploded across Drake's skin and through his skeleton, hurtling him backwards on to the ground. He rolled in pain, his legs refusing to function as he kicked and struggled to stand up.

In the depths of his shock-addled brain, he knew the pain,

recognised it as the same sensation he'd experienced when he'd tried to shoulder-barge the Deathblade Guardian. Only worse. Much, much worse.

It took both War and Pestilence to get him to his feet and keep him there. They were still supporting him when Famine dismounted next to them. He gave the scooter a firm pat on the back of the seat, and it trundled over to a patch of grass on the other side of the road.

Famine looked at the sleeping children and police officers around him, and at the two halves of Dr Black on the pavement at War's feet. "Missed anything?" he wheezed.

Leaving Pestilence to support Drake, War slowly made his way closer to the school gates. He stopped just in front of them and turned his head slowly left and right.

A pale blue glow hung in the air in front of him. It stretched up, down and side to side. It was barely there, barely *anything*. If War hadn't been looking closely, he would never have seen it.

Cautiously, he raised a hand and touched one finger against the glow. A gasp of pain burst through his beard as he drew his arm sharply back. He shook his hand around and clenched it into a fist a few times, never taking his eye off the glow.

"Some kind of magic barrier," he said.

"What, like a force field?" Drake asked. He pulled away from Pest and hobbled over to War. "Can you break through it?"

"I can barely even touch it," the big man replied.

A sudden scream from within the school cut Drake off before he could say anything else. He looked up to the first floor, and caught a brief glimpse of Mel at the window, before a shadow appeared behind her and she was dragged back into the room.

"We have to do something!" Drake yelped. "We have to—"

The Earth trembled beneath his feet. On the other side of the force field, the horses *neighed* and stamped their hooves against the concrete.

A low rumble shook the ground, making them all stagger away from the glowing blue barrier.

"Can I just make it clear," Famine said, "that that wasn't me?"

"Earthquake?" Pest asked. "That's one of the signs! It's

one of the signs of the Apocalypse. Oh, God, what if we're wrong? What if this really *is* the end?"

The ground vibrated again. From inside the barrier there was the sound of falling rubble. Narrow cracks began to split the pavement beneath the horsemen's feet.

"It's not an earthquake," War said grimly. He followed the lines of the cracks. They led all the way back to the school.

"Then what is it?" Drake asked. He was still looking up at the window on the first floor, and so he was the first to notice when it started to move. With a *crack* of snapping concrete, the extension on the front of the school building began to rise slowly up, revealing an enormous chrome construction below.

"What... What is that?" Drake muttered, his eyes following the first storey window as it rose higher and higher into the air, revealing more and more of the metal shape beneath it. "What's happening?"

War groaned. "Something bloody spectacular."

CHAPTER TWENTY-NINE

UNTIL VERY RECENTLY, Drake had never seen a real robot before. But it was safe to say that over the past few days, he'd seen more than his share.

But he had a nagging suspicion that the one before him now would be the *last* one he ever saw.

It rose from the Earth, like a slow-moving rocket with a school balanced on top. Drake didn't realise what it was at first, not until the arms tore their way free of their concrete surround, and hands the size of Panzer tanks helped lift the rest of the metal body out from within the ground.

With a *whinny* of panic, War and Pest's horses bolted. They leaped at the barrier, passing through without any problem, just as the first of the giant robot's feet smashed down on to the ruined tarmac.

Metal groaned as the robot drew itself up to its full, towering height. The dull aluminium cladding of the extension fell away, revealing a head that was the same chrome colour as the rest of the body.

All four horsemen leaned back to look up at the machine. It stood around eighty metres in height, and fifteen or twenty across the shoulders. Decades of dust and soil crumbled away as it held its train-carriage-sized arms out to its sides and stretched its steel tendons.

"There's something you don't see every day," Famine said. He took half a sandwich from beneath a roll of flab, sniffed it cautiously, then began to chew. "What's the plan, then? We running away?"

"No," said Drake firmly. "We're not running away."

"Thank God for that, my feet are killing me," Famine said. He finished his sandwich. "So, what do we do?"

"The horses got out," Drake said. "Maybe the barrier's gone?"

He took a step towards it, only for War to pull him back. "Or, it means things on the inside can get out, but not the other way round." He pointed to a spot just a few centimetres in front of Drake's face. A faint blue light flickered in the air. "It hasn't gone anywhere."

"This is it, then," Pestilence whispered. "This is how the world ends."

Famine shoved a handful of popcorn into his mouth. "I'll be honest, I did *not* see this one coming."

"One giant robot doesn't make an Apocalypse," War said. "Let's just see what happens next."

"No, we have to do something *now*. Mel's up there," Drake said. "We have to..."

His voice fell away. He cocked his head, listening to something he couldn't be sure he had actually heard.

"What's the matter?" asked Pest.

"I thought I... There," Drake said quietly. "Did you hear that?"

"What?" said Famine, chewing thoughtfully. "That buzzing noise?"

"Yeah," said Drake, and at that, the sky went dark.

None of them saw where the billowing mass of silver bodies came from. It was just seconds between the moment Drake heard them and the moment they blocked out the sun. It took even less time for them to swoop down and begin their attack.

There were thousands of them – tens of thousands – each one just eight or nine centimetres long. They came in on metal wings, with pin-like teeth snapping hungrily at everything in their path.

The horsemen were suddenly lost in a cloud of chittering robo-bugs. War swung with his sword. It sparked as a dozen metal bodies ricocheted like bullets off the blade. Drake saw them crash to the ground.

"Grasshoppers?" he said, shouting to make himself heard above the buzzing of mechanical wings. "A swarm of grasshoppers?"

"They're not grasshoppers, they're locusts," Pest cried, in a voice bordering on hysteria. He ducked, as his leather hat was lost to the throng of bodies. "And it's not a swarm. It's a *plague*. Don't you see? It's another sign!"

"Techno-magic mumbo jumbo," War spat, swinging with his sword again and bringing down a few more bugs. "That's all. They're not real signs – he's doing them himself. He's trying to—"

A tightly packed section of the swarm, or plague, or

whatever it was, hit War's chestplate with the force of a cannonball. He stumbled back, struggling for balance, before a second attack took him down.

Drake reached out a hand, but the wings and the teeth and the sleek metal bodies were a hurricane around him, preventing him from moving. He snapped the hood of the robe up over his head and kept low, trying to avoid the locusts, but they were suddenly on his back, their weight forcing him to his knees.

He clawed at the locusts in his hair and saw Famine go down beneath an even bigger pile of winged bodies. War was lying on his back on the ground, punching and kicking, but the things were moving too fast, and there were too many of them, and there was nothing, Drake realised, that they could do.

Through the haze of silver he saw Pest open his mouth, but the horseman's scream was drowned out by the din around them. Pestilence was still on his feet, but only barely. His legs were a heaving mass of silver. His leather jacket was intact, but the clothes beneath it were ragged and torn. He staggered, thrashing around, his eyes wide and panicked and darting from bug to bug to bug as they closed in on him.

"Get off!" Pest's cry was so shrill Drake heard it even above the angry drone of the insects. "Get off, get off, get *off*!"

Drake saw Pest's gloves go up in flames. The smell of burning rubber hit the back of his throat, as green gas sprayed out from Pestilence's fingertips.

Pest stopped screaming. Even the plague seemed to quieten a fraction, as the green fog began to form shapes in the air. They were hazy and indistinct at first, but then the shapes took form. They became tiny numbers, ones and zeroes in the air, circling round and round just beyond Pestilence's reach.

A locust whipped through the cloud of digits and instantly began to fall. From his knees, Drake followed the bug's flight until it clattered on the ground. Another crashed down beside it. Then another, and another.

When Drake looked back up, the air was filled with ones and zeroes. They floated through the swarm, slowly at first, but gaining purpose with each bug they hit.

Another sound replaced the droning of wings. It was the sound of hail on a tin roof, a rattling drumbeat as thousands of metal insects left the sky and arrived, quite abruptly, on the ground.

The weight on Drake's back fell away. He got to his feet

just as War jumped up. The final few locusts clattered to Earth, leaving a great big question hanging in the air.

"What the bloody Hell did you do?" War asked, as he picked robo-bugs from his beard. "I mean, not that I'm complaining."

Pest stared at his hands. He stared at them as if they were loaded weapons, and he couldn't quite remember where the safety catch was.

"I have absolutely no idea," he admitted quietly. "It felt like, like a cold or a flu or something."

"It was a virus," Drake said. Realising it even as the words left his lips. "You made a computer virus."

"A computer virus?" Pest raised his eyebrows. "What's one of them, then?"

But Drake was already looking up at the giant robot, and at the force field that stood between them and it. "I'll explain later," he said. "We have to get in there and stop that thing."

War sheathed his sword. "Right," he said. "But we *can't* get in."

"So, what do we do?" mumbled Famine. He held one of the locusts between finger and thumb, and gave it a cautious sniff.

"There's got to be some way. We have to find a way in. We have to..."

Drake's voice fell away. He knew, in that moment, what he had to do. "I'm Death," he said, as if realising it for the first time. "I'm *Death*."

"We know," Pest said. "You're preaching to the converted there."

"No, I mean *I'm Death*." He looked way up at the school building, shimmering faintly through the force field. "And Death can go anywhere."

He took five purposeful paces backwards, like a footballer preparing to take a penalty kick. "Death can go anywhere," he said, more quietly this time, and for his own benefit.

"You sure about this?" War asked him.

A large part of Drake's brain wasn't sure about this in the slightest, but a small part of it was more certain than it had ever been in its entire life. If he could keep that small part away from the more sceptical larger part for the next twenty seconds or so, everything would almost certainly be fine.

"I can do this," he said. He focused his attention on the mystical barrier, and repeated the words over and over like a mantra. "Death can go anywhere. Death can go anywhere. Death can go anywhere."

He kept chanting as he ran those few paces, picking up speed with every step.

"Death can go anywhere. Death can go anywhere. Death can go anywhere."

The Robe of Sorrows fluttered as he sped towards the force field, still muttering those four words over and over below his breath, faster and faster, like the clattering of a train on the tracks.

"Death can go anywhere Death can go anywhere Death can go anywhere."

He did not close his eyes as the glowing blue wall raced up to meet him. He didn't so much as flinch, even though he very much wanted to. Flinching, he knew, would mean he thought he was about to hit something, and for his idea to work, he had to keep that thought out of his head.

As he approached the barrier, he didn't even jump. Jumping would imply an obstacle in his path, and there were no obstacles in his path. At least, that's what he wanted that little part of his brain to continue believing.

But instinct proved too strong to resist, and Drake raised

his arms in front of his face just as he was about to smack into the force-field wall.

Or rather, that's what he thought was about to happen. In reality, he had run straight through it several paces previously, and was now recoiling in terror from a figment of his own imagination.

"You did it," Pestilence cried. He clapped his gloved hands together, making a muted *thuck-thuck-thuck* sound. "You got through the barrier."

"What? Did I?" Drake asked. "I mean, yeah. No problem."

"Well done!" Famine said. "I think I'll have a nice bun to celebrate." He reached under another fat fold and pulled out something that didn't look very nice. Or, indeed, like a bun.

"Oh, aye, brilliant," War said. "Now what?"

Drake leaned back and looked up at the school building, teetering eighty metres above him on the colossal robot's shoulders.

"I need to get up to... Wait," he said. "What's it doing?"

As he was speaking, one of the chrome giant's arms had begun to move. It rose straight out in front of it, then stopped at a forty-five degree angle to the body. Fingers the size of telephone boxes unfolded, and the metal palm of the robot's hand glowed with a swirling white light.

"I don't like the look of that," Pestilence fretted. He stood behind War, although even this move didn't do much to reassure him.

"What is it?" asked Famine.

As if in answer to the question, the slumbering bodies of the children and police around them began to glow a vibrant shade of blue. Drake watched, hypnotised by the electric glow that now surrounded every one of the sleeping people.

"What's that light?" he asked, getting as close to the barrier as he could without risking stepping back through.

"It's like a big swirling vortex thingy," Pest declared, with the air of authority normally reserved for someone who has at least a vague idea of what they're on about.

"Not that light – *that* light," said Drake. He pointed down to the people on the ground, who were now lit up like a particularly blue Christmas tree.

War, Pestilence and Famine regarded the figures at their feet. They leaned in closer for a better look.

"What light?" Pest said eventually.

"You can't see that?" Drake asked. The lights had become so bright they had merged into one near-blinding glow.

"They're all lit up blue."

"Souls," War said gravely. "My guess is you're seeing their souls. It's something only Death can do."

Drake felt sick. "So, that means, what? He's killing them?"

War's eyes went from sleeping body to sleeping body, as if trying to picture them as Drake saw them. "I don't know," he admitted. "He must be. Unless... What else did that robot-teacher fella say to you? What did he tell you about his plans?"

"Nothing," Drake said. "Just said he was going to get his strength back, and then he was going to do something spectacular."

The part of War's face that Drake could see went pale. "Aw, no," he said. "Aw, no."

"What is it?" Drake asked. "What's wrong?"

"There's only one way he can get his strength back."

"How?"

Drake instinctively ducked, as one of the blue lights became a sphere the size of a bowling-ball, and rocketed upwards past his head. He turned and followed it with its gaze as it was sucked towards the swirling vortex in the palm of the giant robot's hand, like fluff towards a vacuum cleaner, or rugby players to an Indian restaurant.

The ball vanished into the twirling white light, just as two others launched up from the ground at Drake's back.

"Their life force. Their souls," War said. "He's going to eat their souls."

"Ugh, that's *disgusting*," Famine spat. The others turned to look at him. "What?" he said, returning their glares. "Even I have to draw the line somewhere."

"Get your backside up there," War said, oblivious to the balls of light streaking past him with increasing regularity. "You have to take him out before he can power himself back up."

"What'll happen if he does?"

War clenched his jaw. "Anything he wants. Stop him, or Armageddon's happening right here, right now, signs or no bloody signs."

Drake nodded his understanding. "Right," he said, looking up. "Um... how do I get up there?"

"You managed the walking-through-walls thing, so you can manage the horse," War told him. "Whistle. Summon it. Call forth the steed of Death."

He was right, Drake knew. It was now or never. This was his moment.

Curling his index finger and thumb once again, he placed them just inside his mouth, and he blew.

Pffffffff.

"Bugger all," War said, with a not-entirely-surprised sigh.

Drake tried again, but War was quick to stop him. "You're wasting time, and, frankly, you're embarrassing yourself," he told him. "Practise later. Now, get your fingers out of your mouth and start climbing."

"Climbing?" Drake said, but even as he spoke the word, he realised he had no other choice. Mel was up there, in danger. And then there was the whole end-of-the-world thing too. "I'll try to find a way to shut off the shield. When I do, take the robot down. Stop it hurting anyone, or worse."

With the flickering glow of stolen souls dancing eerily around him, Drake raced over to the robot's foot, found a handhold, and slowly, steadily began to climb.

CHAPTER THIRTY

DRAKE FELT LIKE Jack in *Jack and the Beanstalk*, only he wasn't climbing the beanstalk, he was climbing the giant himself.

The metal used in the robot's construction was smooth, but the surface itself wasn't. It was crisscrossed with cables and pitted with rivets. The hexagonal heads of bolts stuck out regularly along the machine's entire length. The effect was like a ladder, reaching all the way up from the ground to the head, far, far above.

He reached for the next handhold, a length of steel cable running almost horizontally across the mechanical thigh. His fingertips found it, brushed against the rough surface, then missed completely as the cable began to move.

No, not the cable, Drake realised. The entire leg.

He felt himself sliding, slipping, swinging left as the leg slowly raised to the right. Frantically, he jammed his foot against a protruding rivet and his knuckles turned white as his grip tightened on the bolt he was clinging to.

He craned his neck, and looked down. The other horsemen were retreating, pulling back as the leg Drake was hanging from came stomping down towards them.

"The kids!" Drake shouted, but his voice was drowned out by the creaking of the metal leg. The other schoolchildren and the police were all still flat on the ground. The souls were still streaking from within them before disappearing into the hand just fifteen or twenty metres away from Drake, but the foot was coming down, down, down and there was nothing Drake could do about it.

He closed his eyes and pressed his face in against the metal, unable to watch what was about to happen next. He was supposed to be the personification of death itself, but he could not – would not – watch everyone die.

There was a *boom* as the foot crunched down on to the ground, and a sudden jolt that almost sent Drake tumbling in the same direction. One of his hands slipped from the bolt and his legs were suddenly kicking against thin air.

Despite all that, he had to look down. He had to know if all those people were dead or—

"Alive," he said, and the word came out as a breathless laugh. The foot had stepped cleanly over them, crushing the police cars instead. A few more souls were sucked from the sleeping teenagers, and Drake suddenly found himself wondering if he were wrong. If the life force was being torn from within them, then maybe they weren't still alive after all.

There was another groaning of metal and the other leg began to lift. The robot had started to walk. Drake looked up. The waist was just half a dozen metres away. He had to get past there before the right leg moved again.

Gritting his teeth, Drake reached for the horizontal cable again, wrapped his fingers round it and pulled.

✢

"Mount up," War commanded, swinging himself into the saddle of the red horse. "Keep close to that big bugger, but don't get too near the barrier."

Pestilence climbed up on to his horse's back and took hold of the reins, ignoring the animal's stress-induced nosebleed.

With a grunt, Famine slid on to the faux leather seat of his scooter and turned the key in the ignition.

"So, what's the plan?" he called.

The robot's left leg slammed down, making the ground tremble and quake. Along the street, half a dozen windows exploded. There were sirens and screaming in almost every direction now, as the town woke up to the fact that a massive robot was about to stomp it to bits.

"Minimise civilian casualties," War barked, sounding more and more like an army commander in the field. "Then, when Drake gets rid of that shield, we take that thing down."

"How?"

"We'll improvise," War said. He flicked his reins and they gave a loud *crack*. "Horsemen," he bellowed. "Let's ride!"

✦

Drake had made it past the waist with seconds to spare. The left leg had now thudded down and the right one was raising. He could see the horsemen below, trying to drive back anyone stupid enough to get too close to the towering machine.

He looked up. In comparison with the rest of its body,

the robot's legs were short and stubby. That meant he hadn't even reached the halfway point yet.

The next handhold swung out sharply as a circular door was thrown open. Clinging to it with both hands, Drake found himself dangling from the hatch as four metal spheres were launched from within it.

He braced himself, expecting the balls to turn on him, but they rocketed away from the robot instead, *swooshing* past one another as they raced in the direction of the horsemen.

"Look out!" Drake cried, but the others were too far away to hear him.

Drake was hanging at the full stretch of his arms, his fingers already beginning to shake with the pressure of his weight and the insistent nagging of gravity. He looked across to the circular hole where the spheres had emerged. The hole formed the mouth of a dark tunnel, running deep into the machine's innards.

He looked up at the fifty or so metres he still had to climb. He looked across at the hole. The decision was easy.

Swinging his legs up, he kicked for the edge of the hole. His heels slammed down into the mouth of the tunnel and he was able to shimmy his legs further into the darkness, as the hatch began to swing closed.

He just managed to whip his fingers away from the edge before the hatch clanged shut, trapping him inside.

"Made it," he breathed, then he listened to his voice echoing over and over again into the distance. Each time it did, it sounded less and less convinced that he'd made the right decision.

"Here goes," he whispered, as he crawled along a dark, narrow passageway, searching for a way up into the robot's head.

✦

"Get back! All of you, get back!" War bellowed. He was zigzagging along the road, waving his sword around, trying to drive away anyone who got too close to the marching robot.

He turned the horse in the direction of a group of onlookers, twenty or thirty metres ahead. They were all pointing at something. Their outstretched fingers started high, then quickly lowered until they were pointing almost directly at War.

The big man turned to see what they were looking at, just as a spinning metal sphere struck him. Thrown backwards, he smacked against the ground, before skidding clumsily across the tarmac.

Growling, War got to his feet, his sword raised. He ran at the sphere, which was hanging in mid-air, not backing away.

WHUMPF!

Another of the spheres slammed into his side, sending him staggering. A cable shot from within the first sphere, a barbed hook at its tip burying itself deep into the back of War's neck.

An electrical current crackled along the wire and War's back arched. Static sparks flickered across his beard as he sunk to his knees, his contracting muscles no longer able to keep him standing.

Even over the electrical buzzing in his head, War heard the panicked scream of Pestilence, and the shocked cry of Famine as more of the spheres closed in to attack.

CHAPTER THIRTY-ONE

PEST'S HORSE KICKED out with its back legs, slamming its hooves against a sphere. It spun like a snooker ball off a side cushion and clipped another of the balls. One of them was sent spiralling up into the air, while the other clattered against the ground, throwing out a spray of angry sparks.

"Famine, War's down!" Pest yelped. "Help him!"

"Bit busy," Famine grunted. He was careening round in circles, his scooter tilting on to two wheels as he tried to outrun another of the robotic orbs.

"Yah!" cried Pest, and his horse raced towards the fallen War. Two of the spheres raced to intercept him, and he dismounted mid-gallop, letting the horse continue on. The spheres didn't react quickly enough. They continued to chase the horse, leaving Pestilence free to pick up War's fallen sword.

"Flippin' Nora, what's that made of?" he winced, as he tried to raise the weapon off the ground. His knees almost buckled as he lifted it with both arms. "Right," he said, using all his strength to raise the blade above his head. He took aim at the sphere that had immobilised War. "Have some of this!"

Pest tried to bring the sword swinging down, but he couldn't summon the energy. His eyes opened wide with surprise as he began to topple backwards, pulled by the weapon's weight.

The sword *clanked* against the pavement as Pest landed in a heap on the ground. Frantically, he tried to get to his feet, but the two spheres that had been chasing the horse had now realised their mistake.

Whirling saw-blades emerged from within both balls as they spun towards him, closer and closer, the saws' teeth chewing hungrily at the air.

Screaming, Pest kicked backwards across the tarmac, his face fixed in a mask of terror. He raised his hands, the shreds of melted rubber still clinging to his fingers.

"Virus thing, virus thing!" he wailed, trying to repeat his

earlier trick. But he had no idea how he'd done it then, and no ones or zeroes were flying from his fingertips now.

With a whine of their blades, both spheres picked up speed and lunged at the fallen horseman. A blur of black collided with one of the spheres, sending it bouncing along the road.

"Gotcha!" Famine cried, skidding his scooter round in a one-eighty degree spin. The sphere's blade retracted, allowing it to roll across the concrete. It hurtled after the scooter, picking up speed with every bouncing roll.

Famine jumped from the moving scooter. Jumping was not something he did often, but, despite the size of him, it was something he did rather well. He sailed through the air, like a wrestler off the top turnbuckle, his arms and legs splayed wide.

His full weight came down on top of the sphere, and kept going until it hit the ground. He lay there, wobbling gently for a few seconds, before he rolled on to his back. A thin oblong sheet of metal remained on the ground where he had landed.

"Get away, get away, get away!"

Famine tried to sit up, but his stomach got in the way. He could only lift his head, could only watch as the spinning blade of the other sphere closed in on Pestilence.

"Pest!" he bellowed. "Look out!"

That, Pest thought, was probably the most pointless thing Famine had ever said, but there was no time to tell him that. There was no time for anything but closing his eyes and holding his hands in front of his face. He hoped he cut open easily. He could imagine nothing worse than the blade having to hack repeatedly at his flesh and sinew as it tried to slice its way through him, but it would be just his bloody luck.

The sphere shattered like a conker as another of the balls smashed down hard against it. Pest looked up to find War standing on trembling legs, sparks dancing along his beard.

The barbed hook was still attached to the back of his neck, but War had managed to grab hold of the wire that tethered him to the sphere. He roared with pain as he swung the ball round in a wide circle above his head, making it *whum-whum-whum* as it looped round and round.

And then, with a vaguely comical *twang*, the cable snapped. The sphere arced through the air before bouncing off the barrier surrounding the approaching robot.

"Shield's still there," War announced. He tore the hook from his neck and stretched his cramped muscles. Then, smoothing down his beard, he retrieved his sword.

The sounds of screaming were getting more distant as people saw sense and started legging it to safety. That was one problem taken care of. Unfortunately, there were plenty more problems where that came from.

Five more spheres hung in the air around them, spinning silently. Doors slid open on the surfaces of each of the balls, as weapons emerged from within them. A buzz-saw. A gun barrel. Something that looked a lot like an industrial drill.

With one hand, War heaved Famine back up on to his feet. The three of them stood there, back to back as the spheres hovered slowly closer.

"Horsemen," War said in a voice that boomed like the sounds of battle. "Let's bust some balls."

✛

Drake ran up stairs and climbed ladders where he could, scaled the walls where there was no other way up. Finally, another ladder led him to a hatch in the ceiling. The hatch lifted up and over, and daylight flooded in. Clambering through, he emerged on to the robot's shoulder.

The right arm stretched down below him like a giant

slide. He peered past it, down to the distant ground where Horsemen-shaped ants battled tiny silver marbles.

A robotic foot thumped down, sending a shockwave through the entire metal structure. Drake wobbled unsteadily for a moment, then found his footing.

The robot's head loomed just above him. He could see the mouth shape, formed by the rows of windows. The two other windows, situated a storey or so above the mouth, looked more like eyes than ever.

The side door, through which Drake and the other horsemen had entered earlier, was sealed over once again with a fresh metal skin. That left only one way to get inside the robot's head.

Drake's eyes went along the row of windows, stopping at the middle where the glass and a chunk of the wall had been smashed away. It looked, he thought, like a missing tooth. Had he stopped to think about it, he would also have realised that it looked like something else.

It looked like a trap.

But he didn't stop, and he didn't think about it. Instead he scrambled up the chrome giant's neck, took hold of one of the narrow metal window ledges, and pulled himself up.

War's sword *whummed* loudly, and a sphere became a number of expensive component parts on the pavement. He spun, following the blade's momentum, and sliced through a gun barrel that had been pointing at Famine's back.

"Have it!" War roared, driving a headbutt into the centre of the ball and cracking the metal shell. Famine's pudgy fingers forced their way in through the gap. His hands pulled in opposite directions, widening the crack just enough for his head to fit through. Opening his mouth wide, Famine lunged and began chomping hungrily on the wires and circuitry within the sphere.

A moment later, he released his grip and the broken ball hit the ground. Famine burped loudly, then licked his lips.

"Tastes like chicken," he announced, as the three remaining balls circled round for another attack run.

Drake swung in through the broken window, slipped on the floor, and landed flat on his back. Luckily, the room was empty, so no one was around to see his embarrassing entrance.

Or so he thought.

"Well, well, well, if it isn't Frosties boy."

"Enjoy your trip, knob 'ead?"

Drake looked up at three spotty scowls. He sprang to his feet and raised his hands, ready for a fight.

"You don't want to mess with me," Drake warned them. He drew himself up to his full height. It wasn't much, but to the tiny bullies he imagined himself looking like a giant. "I'm Death, you know?"

"Yeah, we know," Bingo said with a snort.

"Oooh, scary," laughed Dim.

"Yeah," added Spud. "Oooh, scary!"

"That was them being, what do you call it? Sarcastic," Bingo pointed out. "We're not scared of no Death." His spotty cheeks rose as his mouth twisted into an impossibly wide grin. "We's already dead, ain't we?"

"Yeah, we're as dead as the emu," Dim sniggered.

Drake felt a pang of something. Pity, maybe. "I'm sorry," he said quietly.

"What for?" Bingo snorted. "Our old bodies is dead, but we've got new bodies now, thanks to Mr Franks and Dr Black."

"Yeah, I saw what you can do," Drake said.

Bingo's eyes blazed red. "Oh, you ain't seen nothin' yet!"

The three figures took a synchronised step forward. The room was filled with the sounds of machinery moving. Drake could see some kind of transformation starting to take place, but he could see something else too. Something behind the three boys.

Something that looked, just a little, like a cat.

Drake rolled sideways just as Toxie launched himself at the cyber-bullies. Caught in mid-transformation, they were knocked off balance. There was a panicked cry of "My mum's going to kill me!" and then they were gone, through the hole in the wall, and plunging down towards the ground far below.

Drake heard three brief distant tremors, and he knew the bullies wouldn't be bothering him again.

Toxie, who was looking more and more like a cat by the minute, turned to Drake, sniffed lazily, and said, "Woof."

"Good dog," Drake said. Toxie wagged his tail happily, then sauntered out on to the windowsill and began climbing expertly down the robot's front.

Drake was halfway to the door when the old TV set that

stood on a trolley over by the whiteboard, came on with a *click*.

"That was a stroke of luck," Mr Franks said. "I didn't think they'd stop you, but I thought they'd hold you up longer than that. Still, as you'll have noticed by now, I'm not there. I'm upstairs on the roof, and I've got your girlfriend with me. Look."

The camera panned round, and Drake saw a shock of red hair. Mel was tied by the wrists and ankles to a pole that was hanging precariously over the edge of the roof. She was facing downwards, her hands behind her, her eyes open wide with terror.

Mr Franks' face suddenly filled the screen again in extreme close-up. "I'd rather you didn't come up, but I know you're going to, so why waste my breath?" He winked brightly. "So, see you soon, I guess. I'll try not to drop the redhead, but, well, I'm not going to promise anything, so if I were you – which I sort of was, when you think about it – I'd move fast."

The sound faded.

The screen went blank.

And Drake moved fast.

CHAPTER THIRTY-TWO

RAKE HAD PLANNED to sneak up on to the roof, but Mr Franks was sitting in a deckchair, watching the hatch expectantly. He smiled broadly when Drake's head popped through it.

"There he is!" Mr Franks beamed. "There's the man of the hour. Up you come, join the fun."

He jumped up as Drake stepped out on to the top of the robot's head. "Take a seat," Mr Franks said, gesturing at the deckchair the way a gameshow host's glamorous assistant might gesture at today's star prize.

"No, thanks," Drake said.

Mr Franks put his hands on his hips and nodded. "You're right, you're right. What was I thinking? Sitting down?"

With a sudden jerk he grabbed the back of the folding

chair and hurled it over the edge of the roof. "Boring people sit down, and we're not boring people, are we, Drake? Huh? Am I right?" He looked Drake up and down. "Nice outfit, by the way. Black suits you."

"Mel, are you OK?" Drake asked. He didn't take his eyes off Mr Franks.

"She can't answer you," Mr Franks said. He indicated the gag across her mouth. "She can talk, your girlfriend, can't she? She just would not shut up. It was either gag her, or cut her tongue out."

"It's going to be OK. I'm here to rescue you."

"Aww, you hear that? He's here to rescue you." Mr Franks wiped an imaginary tear from the corner of his eye. "That – if you don't mind me saying? – that's beautiful." He pointed at Drake and mimed shooting him with his finger. "You're a real ladykiller."

The teacher slipped his hands into his pockets and strolled over to a wooden table that had been bolted on to the metal beneath it. An old-fashioned-looking control deck, all knobs and dials and slider switches, hung over the edges of the table on all sides. A spaghetti of wires dangled from the back of the deck, before disappearing into a junction box beneath the table.

A large metal tube, about the circumference of a dinner plate and around half as tall as Mr Franks, rose from the floor beside the desk. A glass dome was mounted on top of the tube, like an upside-down fish bowl. Inside the glass, a living blue light pulsed and heaved.

"Like it?" Mr Franks asked. He pressed a hand against the glass and stroked it gently.

"What are you going to do with them?" Drake asked.

"With what, the souls?" Mr Franks said. He pointed at the glass. "With these souls trapped in here?"

"Yes, what are you going to do with them?"

Mr Franks jumped up and punched the air with his fist. "Then it *does* work!" he cried. "I couldn't be sure because, you know, I can't see souls any more, so I thought, 'Who *can* see souls? Who can I get up here to let me know if this baby works?' and there was only one name I thought of. Can you guess who it was?"

"Me," said Drake. He felt his heart sink. "What now?"

"Now, I'm going to eat them." His face split into a wicked grin and madness blazed behind his eyes. "And when I do, I'm going to get all my old strength back, and then... This is the best bit... Then I am going to split this world in two, Drake. I'm going to split it in two!"

"Why?"

"Why? I thought you, of all people, would know why." He gestured up at the sky. "We're in the Armageddon business, you and I. The end of the world – it's our purpose."

"Everyone will die. *Everyone*."

Mr Franks nodded. "That's the general idea. But listen, it's nothing personal. I'm just following orders. It's my job, after all."

"*Was* your job," Drake reminded him.

"Then consider me freelance." His face darkened. "They told me I could end the world – they *created me* to end the world – and that's exactly what I'm going to do. It's right there, in my contract of employment. 'Begin the Apocalypse.' I'm only following orders. I'm just... bringing forward the schedule a little."

"You're going to decimate the world because you're a *jobsworth*?"

"Not *decimate*, Drake. Didn't your last school teach you anything? Decimate means reduce by ten per cent. I'm not going to decimate the world." He couldn't fight back a self-satisfied smile. "I'm going to *obliterate* it!"

Drake took a step forward. Mr Franks' finger reached for a button on the control desk. "Ah, ah, ah!" he warned. "Look at the pole holding your girlfriend there. Check out the bottom, where it meets the roof."

A bomb, that's what Drake saw. He didn't know how he knew it was a bomb, he just did. It had a certain bomby quality that was unmistakable. "Take another step and she falls," Mr Franks told him. Drake shuffled back, and the teacher's finger relaxed on the button.

He looked Drake up and down, as if seeing him for the very first time. "So, you're the new Death, eh? You're my replacement? I expected something a little more... impressive."

"I guess they thought I was impressive enough to follow you," Drake retorted.

"Ha!" said Mr Franks, without humour. "You think you even come close to matching me? I was Death for a thousand years. I was the longest-serving of all the Deaths."

"Longest serving *so far*," Drake said.

"You don't still think you're going to stop me, do you?" Mr Franks laughed. "I've been planning this for the last five hundred years, putting every element of it into position for the past six decades. I've thought of every last detail. What, you think giant robots build themselves?"

"Yeah, I've been meaning to ask," Drake said. "A giant robot? Isn't that a bit, you know, crap?"

Something that may have been the beginnings of a cringe passed across the teacher's face. "It was the fifties," he explained. "Giant robots were all the rage."

He took a step away from the control deck, thought better of it, then moved back into position beside it. "You know what it's like, sitting around in that shed for a thousand years? No, of course you don't, you've only been there a few days. Maybe you can imagine it, though. Their voices, everything they say, it just becomes this... noise in your head. Like the quacking of ducks. Quack, quack, quack. Quack, quack, quack.

"And then there's the sound of Famine chewing, like some bloated, masticating cow, hour after hour, day after day, chomp, chomp, chomp, continually, on and on."

Mr Franks shook his head, as if trying to drive out the memories. "Pestilence, with his constant whining and complaining and his itching and his flaking and his endless series of spectacular rashes. And War?"

The teacher's voice had been rising throughout his rant. He stopped and brought it back under control. "God, I hated him most of all, strutting around, acting like he was the Big I Am. *I* was supposed to be the leader. *Me!* So why did they always listen to him?"

"Because you're a friggin' headcase?" Drake suggested.

Fury flashed across Mr Franks' face. He looked at Mel. His finger went to the switch on the control deck, but a shout from Drake made him hesitate. "Kill her and I'll kill you!"

The teacher's finger hovered above the button. "Kill me?" he said. "I don't think you would."

"I would," Drake said. "I will. I've... I've killed before."

Mr Franks smiled and shook his head, but his finger withdrew from the button. "No, you see, *me*, I'm a killer. I've killed hundreds of people in the past decade alone. *Thousands*. And why?"

He opened his mouth to answer his own question, then paused. "I don't know, really," he admitted. "Practice, I suppose. I am – *was* – Death, after all. And also because I was bored, and I couldn't face one more bloody game of

Cluedo." He pointed at Drake. "You, on the other hand, have killed what? Half a dozen frogs?"

"Nine," Drake corrected. "I killed nine frogs."

Mr Franks clapped his hands slowly. "Bravo. Truly you are Death incarnate. But, please, let an old hand show you how it *should* be done."

He pushed a slider switch on the control deck and the blue glow inside the dome became agitated. It buzzed and trembled, hurling itself at the glass, but unable to find a way through.

"There's a whole world out there waiting to be destroyed," Mr Franks said. "Let's not keep it waiting any longer."

He reached into his desk drawer and pulled out a large white napkin. He flicked it once to unfold it, then tied it loosely at the back of his neck. "If you'll excuse me," he said, patting his stomach, "I've got a rather pressing lunch appointment."

CHAPTER THIRTY-THREE

DRAKE LOOKED OVER at Mel, hanging above a sheer drop to certain death. He looked at Mr Franks, now adjusting switches and dials on his control deck, making the souls in the bowl quiver and writhe. The teacher hummed quietly below his breath as he worked, a song so ancient no other human alive had heard it.

Slowly, Drake slid one foot a few centimetres across the floor. The thudding of the robot's footsteps had stopped, which meant that the robot itself had stopped. This was a pity because the sound of the footfalls would have disguised the faint *squeak* Drake's own foot made as he inched it across the metal.

"One millimetre closer and your girlfriend drops," Mr Franks told him. He looked up and fixed Drake with a glare.

"You look tense. Relax."

Drake slunk back a pace.

"You still don't look relaxed. You look like someone who's about to attempt a daring, last-minute rescue, and that would be stupid."

Drake let his shoulders sag and his arms hang limply at his sides. He stuffed his hands into the robe's deep pockets. "That better?"

"Much," Mr Franks replied. He turned his attention back to the control deck. Beside him, the glass dome was filled with an angry blue fire. "I'm doing you a favour when you think about it, Drake. I'm giving you the opportunity to fulfil your purpose. An opportunity that was taken from me. You should be thanking me."

"Don't hold your breath."

Drake's fingers brushed against something in his right pocket. He felt for the edges, trying to figure out what it was. Round. Hard. Then his finger pricked against something sharp and he knew at once what to do.

"Those frogs we were talking about," he said, surprising Mr Franks and getting his attention.

"What about them?"

"You should've seen them. All trapped in that tank, stressing out, becoming more and more agitated. I could see they were scared. That's why I did what I did."

"Sounds wonderful," Mr Franks said. "What's your point?"

"I didn't kill them on purpose. I let them go," Drake said, "but they were too frightened. Too panicked. I tipped over the tank and they knocked over a Bunsen burner and do you know what happened next?"

"They all burned alive?"

"Well, yes, but before that," Drake said. "Do you know what happened right before that?"

Mr Franks shook his head. "Go on."

"Chaos," said Drake. He pulled his hand from his pocket and brought it back sharply. "Complete and utter chaos."

With a cry of triumph, Drake hurled the badge at the glass dome. The world seemed to lurch into slow motion as the words 'I AM 4' flipped, end over end over end, on a direct collision course with the glass.

Mr Franks' reactions were quick, but not quick enough. He made a dive for the badge, but his fingers couldn't quite find it. It passed by him and struck the soul bowl dead centre.

And then it bounced harmlessly off, and landed on the metal floor with a faint *chink*.

There was silence for a moment, broken only by a sharp, sudden laugh from Mr Franks. Drake searched his pockets, hoping to find something else to throw, but painfully aware that he wouldn't.

"Wow!" Mr Franks cried. "What a throw! That was brilliant. Just *brilliant*! For a horrible moment there I thought it was actually going to work! I thought you were actually going to ruin everything."

He chuckled and this time the tears he wiped from his eyes were genuine. "But no," he said. "You blew it. Game over, kid. Nice try."

Krik.

The smile fell from Mr Franks' face.

Ka-rick.

Drake watched as a hairline crack spread across the surface of the dome. Inside, the trapped souls were hurling themselves against the glass, pushing up and out in their panic to be free. It was the frogs all over again.

Ka-RACK.

Mr Franks' eyes went wide as the glass dome shattered.

"Oh… crap," he muttered, and then his world descended into chaos.

Drake could see the souls swooshing and swooping around the teacher, batting and buffeting him this way and that. The teacher, however, couldn't see a thing. He flailed out wildly at invisible foes, throwing wild punches and wilder kicks that took him further and further away from the control deck.

Ducking a streaking blue orb, Drake crossed to the controls. He looked over them, trying to figure out what all the buttons and dials and switches and faders and knobs actually did. He could feel Mel's eyes on him, wide open and terrified. He would get her down. In just a few seconds, he would get her down, and she would be safe. But first…

He had to read all the labels three times before his racing brain found the one it was looking for. He flicked a little black switch. There was a sound like a faint sigh, and a sudden wind pushed him back from the control deck.

"The barrier!" Mr Franks wailed. He swatted at where he thought a soul might be and stumbled across to the desk, the wind shoving hard at his back. "What have you done to my barrier?"

Drake ducked against the howling winds and raced to

reach the controls before the teacher did. He had to protect the switch, had to prevent Mr Franks from reactivating the force field.

With a cry of triumph, Drake's hand clamped down over the switch, blocking it from the teacher's reach. His victory was short-lived, though, when he realised that Mr Franks hadn't been going for *that* button.

There was a *click*.

There was a *bang*.

There was a *scream*.

And the metal rod, with Mel attached, detached from the roof and disappeared over the edge.

"No!" Drake bellowed as, without a second thought, he rushed to the edge and hurled himself after her.

The air roared in his ears, louder than anything he'd ever heard in his life. He plummeted head-first, his arms tucked in by his sides, his feet pointed back up towards the roof so as to make his body as streamlined as possible.

Mel had fallen free of the pole she had been tied to. She twisted and spun through the air, flipping and twirling as she plunged towards a very messy death on the hard ground below.

Ever so slowly, the gap between them was closing. Drake felt a surge of hope. *I'm going to make it,* he thought. *I'm going to make it!*

✦

"He's not going to make it," Pest yelped. "He's not going to make it!"

He and the other horsemen had seen the flicker as the barrier had fallen, then heard the blast, way up high, as the bomb at the base of Mel's pole had detonated. They had seen her fall, and had watched as Drake launched himself after her. The gap between the distant falling figures was narrowing. It was definitely narrowing.

But it wasn't narrowing quickly enough.

✦

Drake plunged. The ground was racing up to meet Mel. She'd never survive the fall. He wasn't even sure if he would, but at least he had a fighting chance. He had to reach her, had to catch her, but with each metre that passed the chances of him doing that grew smaller and smaller.

He brought his arms out in front of him, hands together

above his head, so his body almost formed the shape of a missile. The robe billowed out behind him like the cape of some dark, avenging superhero.

The robe. The robe was slowing him down!

Wriggling furiously, he untangled himself from the heavy cloak. It fluttered upwards as the wind caught it, and Drake felt himself speed up. The whistling air stung his eyes as the gap between him and Mel began to close more rapidly.

His grasping fingers brushed against her clothes. His arms went round her. He pulled her in close, twisted until he was beneath her and then, with a *boom*, they both hit the ground.

CHAPTER THIRTY-FOUR

DRAKE BLINKED BOTH his eyes. He could do that, at least. That was something.

He was lying on his back. Mel was lying on his front, his arms holding her against him. The robe was on the ground beneath them. He didn't have the energy to try to figure out how. He looked up and saw three concerned faces looking down at him.

"Oh, thank God," Pest said, letting out a breath he had been holding on to for a long time. "You're OK."

"Welcome back," War said. "Good catch."

"Biscuit?" asked Famine, holding out a packet of digestives.

Pestilence and War looked at the fat man in quiet amazement. "Well, there's a first," Pest said. He reached for the packet. "I'll have one, if it's going."

"Shove off," Famine grunted, pulling the packet back. "I wasn't asking you. I was asking Drake and his lady friend."

"I'm OK, thanks," Drake said. He tried a laugh. It didn't hurt *too* badly. "What about you, Mel?"

Mel did not answer.

"Mel?"

Drake craned his neck so he could look at her. Her eyes were closed. The muscles in her face were slack. "Mel?" Drake said again, and he could hear the desperation in his own voice this time.

"Get her on her back," Famine said, nudging War. "Check her pulse."

Drake scrambled to his feet as Mel was lifted off him. He watched, saw nothing else, as War pressed two fingers against Mel's throat, then gave a single slow shake of his head.

"N-no, but I saved her," Drake stammered. "I caught her. I saved her."

Pest took hold of his arm, holding him back. "The fall itself..." he said softly. "Humans, they're fragile. The fall itself could've done it. There's nothing you could have done. There's nothing anyone could do."

Famine licked his rubbery lips, then wiped the saliva away with the back of his arm. "Yes, there is," he said. "Rules of First Aid. Step one, check for dangers." All but Drake glanced up at the robot. "We won't count that one," Famine decided. "Step two—"

"Just hurry up!" Drake cried.

"All right, all right, keep your hair on," Famine muttered, as he dropped to his knees. He opened and closed his mouth a few times, warming up, then he tilted back Mel's head, clamped his lips over hers, and blew.

One breath, that was all it took. She coughed, spluttered, sat up, stared, then slumped back down again, her eyes closing as she fell. War checked again for a pulse. This time, he nodded.

Famine licked a finger, pressed it against the side of his face, and made a hissing sound, like water becoming steam.

"She reacted quickly to that," War said.

Pest shuddered. "Do you blame the girl?"

Drake was down on his knees. He hugged Famine. Or rather, he hugged a small percentage of Famine. The rest would have to wait.

"Mel," he said, but the word came out as a sob. He placed

a hand on her face. He could feel her moving beneath his touch, as her breath came and went. "You're going to be OK," he whispered. He became aware that his cheeks were wet with tears. "You're going to be OK."

Her eyelids flickered, then opened. "Hey, Chief," she croaked. "What... what happened?"

Drake resisted the urge to glance at Famine. "Trust me," he said. "You don't want to know."

She tried to sit up, but pain twisted her face and she lay back down. Her eyes swam for a moment, but she forced them to focus on Drake's face. "Did you stop him?"

"Not yet."

"Then what are you waiting for? We had a deal, remember?"

Drake nodded and smiled grimly. "I remember."

From the noise she made, Drake knew it hurt, but Mel forced her head and shoulders up until she could kiss him on the cheek. "Go get him, Drake," she said.

"Can we hurry this up, do you think?" War muttered. "I'm three seconds away from puking in my own beard."

"Oh, stop teasing him," Pest said, slapping War on the arm. "Can't you see? The boy's in love!"

"*What?*" Drake spluttered, his face reddening.

"Listen, if you ever need any advice, Drake, come and see me," Famine told him, then he winked and tapped his nose. "I know a thing or three."

"Will everyone *please* shut up?" War growled. "We've still got the big metal bugger there to deal with, in case you hadn't noticed."

Drake joined War in staring up at the mechanoid. "Any ideas? Could you, like, chop its feet off or something?"

"Doubt the sword will get through that," War said.

"I could eat it," Famine suggested. "But it might take a while," he admitted.

"We have to do *something*," Pest said.

But the robot did something instead. Its foot lifted into the air as it began to stride forward once more. The horsemen watched the foot pass above them, before it slammed down on top of a parked car, sending all four tyres rolling along the road.

The machine paused then, before its arms raised out in front of it, first one, then the other. It twisted at the waist, then its head jerked round until it was facing the wrong way.

With a loud *clank*, the head and the torso snapped back to face the front again, just as the other leg lifted into the air.

"What's it playing at?" War growled. "It's going mental."

"It must be the souls," Drake said, peering up. He could see blue streaks looping around at the top of the robot's head. "I set the souls free. They're running riot up there. They must've damaged the controls. We need to bring it down before it trashes the whole town."

"But how?" Pest asked.

Drake's mind raced. There was something else about his two visits to Sunday School. Something else that had been covered in the puppet show. A sort of mini-show, before the Jesus and the Leper main event. What was it? What was it?

"Daniel and Goliath!" he cried.

"You mean David and Goliath," War said.

"Daniel, David, whatever," Drake said. He looked across to one of the spheres that had fallen during the battle. War followed his gaze. Realisation slowly dawned across his bearded face. "Can you do it?" Drake asked.

With barely a grunt, War picked up the sphere. "With my eyes shut."

"Fire away," Drake said. "Aim for the head, like Daniel did."

"David!"

"Whatever! Just throw it."

War balanced the ball in one hand, then pressed it against the side of his hairy cheek. Like a shot-putter, he launched the ball skyward. They all watched as it flew up, up, up towards the robot's head.

"Easy," War said, flexing his muscles. "It's home and dry."

There was a distant *bang* as the ball smashed against the robot's thick shell.

"Look out!" Drake cried. A rain of metal and wire and dark red liquid fell to Earth around them.

Pest stared at the falling liquid in horror. "Blood," he whimpered. "A rain of blood. Another sign!"

"It's not blood," War said, touching the stuff with his fingers and smelling it. "It's engine coolant."

"Coolant?" Drake muttered.

"Must be to stop the spheres overheating," War said, wiping his gloves on his trousers.

"Looks like blood to me," fretted Pest.

"It's *not* blood!" War bellowed. "And it's *not* the Apocalypse."

"It might be if we can't stop that thing," Drake said. The robot took another thunderous step forward. "Can you try again?"

"The balls aren't solid enough," War told him. "It's no use. We need something heavier."

"We don't have anything heavier!"

There was the sound of a throat being cleared. "Me."

Drake, War and Pestilence turned. Famine stood behind them, looking a little embarrassed. He smiled uncertainly. "Throw me."

"Don't be daft," Pest said. "It's too dangerous."

"It's a long fall from up there," War said. "There's no saying you'd survive."

Famine's round shoulders shrugged. "There's no saying I won't. Besides, Drake did."

"Aye, but you've... got a bit more weight behind you," War said diplomatically.

Something like a laser blast scorched from the robot's outstretched hand and a petrol station a hundred metres away became a ball of flame.

"Better hurry," Famine said.

"There's got to be another way," Pest protested. He had found his leather cap again, and was holding it in both hands, nervously fiddling with the peak. "There's got to be."

"Well, we could throw you, but the wind'd carry you

away," Famine told him. Then he smiled, warmly and patted his friend on the shoulder as he passed him.

"Are you sure about this?" asked Drake.

"Not really," Famine admitted. He turned to War. "Let's get it over with, eh?"

War creaked his neck and stretched his muscles. "Aye," he said. "Let's do it."

He caught Famine by the back of the neck and the waistband of his trousers.

"Brace yourself," he warned, as he began to spin like a hammer thrower, twirling the fat man out in a wide circle.

"Good luck," Famine blurted, then he very suddenly felt lighter than he had ever felt before. The ground and the other horsemen fell away. Famine laughed. He was flying, soaring, rising up and up like some beautiful, elegant bird.

WHANG!

Famine's arms and legs formed a sort of squidgy star-shape as his body struck the head of the robot. He barely had time to utter an "ooyah" before he slid down what passed for the mechanoid's forehead, then began the long plunge back down to Earth.

He hit the ground like a meteorite, throwing up chunks

of rubble and debris in all directions. He was very relieved that it hurt. That meant he wasn't dead. Not quite, at least.

His head went light. The world turned grey at the edges. The last thing Famine saw before he passed out was an eighty-metre tall robot ever so slowly begin to topple backwards.

CHAPTER THIRTY-FIVE

DRAKE HEARD THE sound of cheering or screaming in the distance, he couldn't tell which. Then he heard the indescribable sound of a giant robot falling on to a row of houses, and then, for the next few seconds, he heard nothing but the ringing in his own ears.

Drake hadn't seen him move, but Pest was already scrabbling down the side of the crater caused by Famine's fall.

"He's alive!"

Even over the ringing in his ears and the sound of settling debris, Drake heard War sigh with relief.

"He's alive, but he's hurt," Pest cried. "Someone fetch me a Kit-Kat."

"We did it," Drake said, looking over at the fallen robot.

War nodded. "Aye. Looks like it," he said. He nodded

towards where Mel was still sitting on the ground. "Go and check on her. I'll help that pair."

Drake didn't hang about. He hurried over to the side of the road and knelt down by Mel. She managed a smile for him, and he gave one right back.

"It's over," he said, taking her hand and squeezing it. "We stopped him. It's over."

Her smile widened, until it became the crinkle-nosed grin Drake would never, ever tire of seeing. "Good work," she said. "I knew you could do it." She thought about this. "Well, *hoped*, at least."

Down in the crater, Pest was cradling Famine's head. He didn't even appear bothered by the strings of drool hanging from the fat man's open mouth, even when they began dripping on to his leather chaps.

War slid down the last few metres of the hole and nudged Famine with his boot. "Right, wake up," he said.

"Steady on," Pestilence complained. "He's hurt. Don't be so rough. You can't just *make* him wake up."

"Oh, look," said War loudly. "I've found a cake."

Famine's eyes opened. "Cake?"

War smirked. He reached into his pocket and pulled out

an individually wrapped muffin. Famine took it and ate it, without bothering to unwrap it first.

"Did I do good?" Famine asked, as the other horsemen helped him to his feet.

"You did good," War said, nodding.

"You were wonderful," Pest enthused. He and War took an arm each and led Famine up the incline and on to the pock-marked road. They waved over to Drake. Pestilence began to say something.

That was when it hit them.

Drake didn't see *what* hit the horsemen. The light was so blinding it forced his eyes to close, but even that couldn't stop it burning into his retinas. He heard Mel hiss with the pain and shock of it.

When the light faded and Drake could open his eyes, War, Famine and Pestilence were face down on the ground, motionless.

Something moved in the pit behind them. Drake watched in horror as a twisted metal monstrosity *clanked* up on to the street.

It had Mr Franks' face, but the rest of it was machine. Hydraulics hissed as it marched forward a few paces, each thunderous footstep driving a new pothole into the road. "Robotic exo-skeleton," Mr Franks announced. "Now I *know* you weren't expecting that."

An arm rose. The palm of the robotic hand glowed a swirling white. Drake heard Mel gasp, turned and saw a blue light illuminate her from within. She sagged too quickly for him to catch her. She collapsed to the pavement as her soul streaked past Drake and was swallowed by the light.

"No," Drake cried. "No!"

Mr Franks licked his lips. "Mmm, tasty, tasty!" he cackled. "That one's going to be a meal all by itself."

"Give her back," Drake bellowed. He ran at the teacher. "Let her go!"

Mr Franks reached down and grabbed something from the ground. Something *whummed* towards Drake's face. Drake twisted, but not fast enough. He felt his cheek split open and his blood fell like rain upon the ground.

"Ooh, that looks nasty," Mr Franks grinned. He raised War's sword triumphantly. The point drew a figure of eight in the air just a few centimetres from Drake's nose.

"Give me back her soul, or I'm going to kill you," Drake growled.

"See, this is how it should be!" Mr Franks cried. His eyes blazed with excitement. He was loving every minute of this. "Thrills, spills, drama, adventure. That's what being a horseman should be about, not sitting in a shed for a thousand years playing Snap. I should have ended the world centuries ago."

"You're not going to end the world. We stopped you," Drake reminded him.

"Oh, come on, Drake, you think I didn't have a back-up plan?" He flexed the hydraulic muscles of the metal suit. "Mystical battle armour," he crowed. "What do you think? Does everything the big robot did, but in an all-new slimline package. You were right, the giant robot was a little on the old-fashioned side, but this? This is the future."

"I'll tear it to pieces, with you inside."

"Them's fighting words!" Mr Franks laughed. With one robotic arm he reached round to his back. A long, loosely wrapped bundle of blue polythene landed on the ground at Drake's feet. "So, let's do this properly. Let's settle it. A fight," he beamed, "to the *Death*."

Not taking his eyes off the teacher, Drake unfolded the bundle. A long-handled scythe rolled out. Its blade looked brand new, but Drake somehow sensed that the weapon was as old as time itself.

"So, you're the one who took it."

"The Deathblade," Mr Franks announced. "Pick it up. Embrace your destiny. And then, I'm going to kill –" he breathed in deeply through his nose – "*everyone*."

The wooden handle vibrated gently beneath Drake's grip as he hoisted the Deathblade up. It stood taller than he did, but it felt almost weightless in his hands.

"Not if I kill you first," Drake said.

"Man, I love this! It's so... *exciting*!" Mr Franks cackled. "OK then, Drake, try to kill me. Try to save your girlfriend," he said. With a click of his heels, two compact jet-engines unfolded from the backs of his metal-clad legs. "Catch me if you can!"

With a *roar* from his rocket-boots, Mr Franks propelled himself vertically upwards towards the clouds far, far overhead.

Drake didn't stop to think. His hand was moving before his brain had fully realised what was happening. He curled his thumb and index finger. He put them in his mouth, and he whistled. Finally, he whistled, long and shrill and loud.

And he heard, as it were, the noise of thunder.

CHAPTER THIRTY-SIX

THE SONIC BOOM whipped up the air around Drake. He didn't flinch, not even when the horse tore from the air directly in front of him.

Its front hooves came down hard on the ground, but they didn't make a sound. Its back hooves also fell silently on to the tarmac surface of the road. The horse reared up on to its hind legs, and Drake realised it was bigger than even War's mighty steed.

War had called it 'the pale horse', and it was pale, but not in the way Drake had been expecting. It wasn't so much pale in terms of colour, as pale in terms of *solidity*. Light flowed through it, bending and warping as if passing through a crystal.

The animal wasn't completely transparent, though. Swirls

of living white heaved deep beneath its glassy skin, forming patterns that shifted and whirled every time it moved. When it stood still, as it did now, it could be mistaken for an ice sculpture.

There was no saddle on the horse's back, and there were no reins with which to hold on. Neither of those things made Drake hesitate. In one leap he was sitting on the animal's broad back, the Deathblade clutched in his right hand.

He had expected the horse to be cold, like ice, but it felt neither cold nor warm beneath him. It just felt... there.

Drake didn't give the horse any command. He didn't say anything to make it take to the air. He just thought the instruction and the horse obeyed. *Up*, he thought, and up the horse went, moving swiftly and silently in a steep uphill curve.

The faster the horse moved, the less tangible it became. It no longer resembled an ice sculpture. Now it was a horse-shaped cloud, a silvery vapour trail billowing out in its wake.

Up it went, higher and higher, until the ground was little more than a distant memory. They were running almost straight up now, but Drake was having no problem staying on the horse's back, despite the oncoming wind and gravity's insistent pull. It was as if he and the horse were one creature, inseparable until he decided otherwise.

Over the howling of the wind, Drake heard another sound. The horse banked right, just as the roar of engines filled the air. The robot battle armour whistled by them, performed an impossibly tight turn, then streaked back in their direction.

Drake swung with the Deathblade. There was a *ching* of metal hitting metal, and a bolt of angry lightning ripped across the sky.

Mr Franks drew back War's sword. Red fire crackled along the length of its blade. It lit up his face, illuminating the madness that danced behind his eyes. "Nice horse," he said. "Had it long?"

He lunged again with the sword. The Deathblade twirled in Drake's hand. Was he moving it, or was it moving him? He couldn't quite say. The hooked blade *clanked* against the side of the sword, knocking Mr Franks' aim off.

More lightning exploded and the teacher leaped back, his rocket-boots blasting him out of harm's way. They both lunged again, hacking and slashing with their weapons as they climbed higher and higher into the sky. Each time the weapons met, fingers of electricity clawed at the air around them.

"I've got this problem, Drake," Mr Franks said. He had stopped attacking for the moment, but was still moving upwards. The horse trotted across the sky, maintaining the distance between them. "At first I thought it was just this minor irritation, but, well, it's got bigger, and it just refuses to go away. It's you, in case you were wondering."

"I wasn't," Drake told him.

"I was trying to be nice to you. I wanted you free to fulfil your destiny when Armageddon all kicks off." The teacher's face filled up with contempt. "And it will all kick off. You see, you think you've stopped it, but you haven't. You can't prevent the end of the world, Drake. It's inevitable."

"There's only one thing that's inevitable," Drake replied. "And I'm it."

Lunging wildly, he swung the Deathblade in a wide arc. It sliced through part of a robotic arm, and a spray of red coolant pumped out. The liquid distracted Drake. He didn't see the other exo-skeleton arm come up sharply. A fist the size of a breeze block went *whump* against Drake's chin, and he discovered that he could, in fact, be separated from the horse.

The town was spread out below him like a toy village as he plunged towards it. He could see the roofs of houses. He could see his back garden. And there, lying among it all, was the giant robot the horsemen had defeated together.

The wind seemed to laugh as it howled past his ears. Gravity's pull felt stronger than ever. Drake clung tightly to the Deathblade, as if it could somehow slow his descent, or stop his fall completely.

A metal fist *clanged* against his cheek, widening the split and sending blood spraying up behind him. He tried to twist, but there was nothing to push against. He cried out in pain as a robotic foot slammed against his lower back, and a white-hot jet-engine flame scorched his skin.

He hacked with the scythe, flailing it behind him. Mr Franks dodged easily. Hydraulics *whirred* and an alloy elbow was driven hard against the base of Drake's skull.

The force of the blow flipped him. He spun until he was facing the right way, standing up as he fell down towards the now not nearly so distant ground. A flash of red fire sliced towards him. He held up the Deathblade and War's sword smashed against the blade.

A jagged streak of electricity tore down at them from

above, striking the weapons at the same time. They both watched helplessly, as the sword and the scythe were ripped from their hands, and sent tumbling down through the clouds.

"Now look what you've done!" Mr Franks roared. "Now how am I supposed to kill you? The fall? I doubt that'll be enough."

He looked up. A deranged grin spread across his face, and a metal hand caught hold of Drake. Rockets flared on the battle armour's feet, and they began to climb, straight up at eye-watering speed.

"It's been fun, hasn't it?" the teacher hollered. "You and me. All of *this*. It's been fun. But now I need you out of the way. The sword could've killed you, but now I've lost that, so you've forced me to improvise."

A clear Perspex visor snapped down over Mr Franks' head. "I still need to breathe," he explained. "Until I eat your girlfriend's soul, at least. But you? You're a horseman. Breathing's optional."

Drake had no idea what the madman was on about. "So?"

"Look up."

They had been climbing at an incredible rate. Drake

raised his eyes and saw that the blue sky had become a haze of colours. It looked as if the fabric of the heavens had been stretched out, pulled so thin that he could see the stars shining through it.

"I'm ending the world," Mr Franks cackled, as he saw the moment of realisation spread like a rash across Drake's face. "But, lucky for you, you're not going to be on it."

Drake grabbed at the battle armour. A shock jolted through him, but he kept clawing, kept trying to find a way of pulling the helmet open, of tearing the exo-skeleton apart.

A glug of red coolant slicked his fingers and he lost what little grip he had on the armour. He heard Mr Franks laugh, even over the whistling of the wind, but his attention was fixed on the blood-like liquid.

He thought back to the cave of the Deathblade Guardian, and to the cupboard in Dr Black's room. Air conditioning. Climate control. The engine coolant dribbled from his fingertips, and everything clicked into place.

They began to rise through a bank of cloud, which had appeared as if from nowhere. A horse-shaped section of the vapour suddenly became solid beneath Drake, and their impossibly quick ascent stopped impossibly quickly.

Drake took a moment to look around. He could see the curvature of the Earth stretching out far, far below. He could see the colours of the upper atmosphere, swirling like the surface of a giant bubble. He could see the stars, above and around them, and he could hear... nothing at all. Mr Franks was speaking – shouting – but Drake could not hear a sound.

There was no air, but neither Drake nor his horse required it. Drake looked down at the world spread out below him. It would not end today.

Ignoring the shock of pain, he took hold of Mr Franks' metal frame. He didn't even need to think the next command. The horse moved all by itself.

Down they went, plunging through the atmosphere, faster even than they had climbed. The silence ended with a sudden *boom*, and the sounds of hooves and wind and screaming filled Drake's ears.

The metal of the battle armour went orange, then red, then white as the heat generated by their re-entry into the atmosphere began burning the suit up. Heat. That was the key. That was the weakness.

"Stop!" Mr Franks pleaded. But Drake did not stop. He rode, not across the sky, but straight down, ushering in one very specific, localised Apocalypse.

The heat was intense. Drake could feel it scorching against his skin, but it didn't burn him, *couldn't* burn him.

"Give me her soul back," Drake snarled. "Let her go."

Mr Franks tried to swing with a wild punch, but the heat was making the armour seize up. His fist creaked to a stop several centimetres from its target.

"Let her go, or you die!"

Mr Franks's eyes were wide with terror, but he was hanging on to his defiance. "You won't do it. You're not a murderer."

"No," Drake agreed. "Murderers can be stopped. Death can't. Not by burning, not by falling, not by *you*!"

"You won't do it!"

"Yes," said Drake. "I will." He released his grip. A look of puzzled terror crossed Mr Franks's face and he suddenly found himself freefalling.

Down, Drake thought, and the horse raced after the plummeting teacher, keeping pace, but making no attempt to intercept him. Drake listened to Mr Franks's screams all the way down to the ground.

The madman closed his eyes and prepared himself for the end as the tarmac rushed up to meet him. But he did not hit it. At least, not right away. A firm hand caught him by a robotic ankle, stopping his skull splattering like an egg on the concrete.

"Well, well, well, look who dropped in," War growled. He opened his hand and the armour, with Mr Franks inside, clattered down on to the ground.

Mr Franks looked up to see War, Famine and Pestilence glaring down. War's sword was back in the giant's hand, the tip of the blade held just centimetres from the teacher's face.

"Oh God," Mr Franks groaned. "Not you three."

"Lovely to see you too," Pest said. "We really *mustn't* do this again some time."

There was a moment of ominous silence, when even the blaring of the police sirens died away, and Drake's horse touched down beside them. The other three horsemen stepped aside as Drake strode over, pausing only to pick up the fallen scythe. Even without the Robe of Sorrows, he looked every inch the embodiment of Death.

"Give me back her soul," he commanded, in a voice like the tolling of a funeral bell.

"You want it?" Mr Franks coughed. "You're going to have to kill me to get it."

Without a word, Drake raised the scythe and angled the point towards the teacher's head. "That's it, boy," Mr Franks hissed. "What are you waiting for? Do it. Kill me. Become the Death you are."

Drake shifted his grip on the handle. He chose a spot in the centre of Mr Franks's chest.

"Come on, what are you waiting for? Do it," Mr Franks snarled, and Drake saw the teacher's teeth were coated in blood. "Finish me; do it!"

Without a word, Drake brought the Deathblade down sharply. There was a sound of tearing metal and Mr Franks screamed briefly before he realised he was still very much in one piece.

The armour fell in two, like a peanut shell splitting open. From within the cables and circuitry, a blue glow began to flicker. Drake alone watched as the glow rose into the air, forming a pulsating egg shape. And then, it was gone.

Over by the side of the road, Mel made a sound between a sneeze and a scream. Then she sat bolt upright, her eyes wide. "Wow," she muttered. "That was... interesting."

"She's alive!" Pest cried. "You did it!"

"That's one problem solved," Famine said. He gave the teacher a kick. "What are we going to do with him?"

"Yeah, what are you going to do with me?" Mr Franks demanded.

"Leave him there," War shrugged. He studied the blade of his sword for a moment, shook his head, then slipped it into the sheath across his back.

"You can't leave me here!" Mr Franks looked pointedly to his arms and legs, which were still trapped within the twisted wreckage of the armour. "I can't move."

"Good, then you can explain everything to the police," Pest said.

"The police?" Mr Franks spluttered. "But... but that's for *humans*."

"Yes, but you *are* human now, aren't you?" Pestilence said. "Your choice, no one else's. I'd imagine the police will want to ask you a lot of questions about giant robots and the like."

"And then, I'd imagine, they'll lock you up," Famine added. "With other humans. Violent ones."

"You can't leave me," Mr Franks cried. "What about all those times we had? We were a team. Right?"

"I can see your lips moving," Drake said. "But all I can

hear is this noise. Like the quacking of ducks. *Quack-quack-quack*."

Sirens screamed just a few streets away. War looked over to the horses gathered together near Famine's mobility scooter.

"We'd better get a shifty on," he said. "Don't want to be here when the Bobbies arrive."

Drake crossed to Mel. She put her arms round him and they hugged until the sounds of the sirens were too close for comfort. "We'd better go," he said. "Are we... OK?"

Mel looked up at the ice sculpture of a horse behind her. She looked back at Drake. "We're OK," she said, and then she kissed him for the third time that day. Not that he was counting.

They climbed on to the horse. War was already sitting on his, while Famine waddled across to his scooter. Only Pestilence remained behind.

"You coming?" Drake asked.

"Yeah, just a second," Pest told them. He looked down at Mr Franks, pinned beneath the weight of the robotic battle suit. "Quick question," Pestilence said brightly. "I was just wondering, with you being so clever and everything..."

He raised his gloveless hands and brought them closer to

the teacher's face. "Have you ever heard of Guinea Worm Disease?"

Drake felt Mel's arms go round him. He placed his hands over hers, just as War took hold of his own horse's reins.

"Ready?" the bearded giant asked.

"Ready," said Drake. "Oh, but, I was thinking..."

War glared at him expectantly. "First time for everything, I suppose."

"Next week sometime, once everything's settled down, if you fancy – and if we don't, you know, get cast into Hell for not doing our jobs properly – I thought that maybe we could, I dunno, go fishing?"

War looked off into the distance, as if suddenly able to see some previously unnoticed future spread out there, just beyond the horizon. "Aye," he said, at last. "Why not?"

Then he dug in his heels, flicked the reins, and the Four Horsemen of the Apocalypse rode across the sky and made their way home.

EPILOGUE

HE LEAVES THE plains of the afterlives behind and arrives like a dark, creeping fog in a neatly cropped circle of grass. It is midnight, the dead of night. This is not unusual. To him, it is *always* midnight.

A square construction stands before him. Although he has never seen this place before, he has felt it, sensed it, many times over.

The shed. At last, he has reached the shed. He has reached the moment of his destiny.

Like a drop of black oil he oozes across the grass, past the flowerpots and up to the entrance. His shape shifts, his living cloak wraps round his solidifying form, and a hand that is no more than bleached bone raps three times on the wooden door.

There is a sound from inside. A clatter and then a *thud*. A thin man appears, his body dressed in white, his hands clad in a thin second skin.

"Hello?" the man asks, surprised, but not shocked by his skeletal appearance. "What can I do you for?"

The words hiss out of their own accord. Words he has waited to speak since being brought into existence. Words he was created to speak.

I aaaammm Deeeeeaaathhh...

The thin-faced man looks him up and down. "Oh," he says. "So *you're* supposed to be... And he's not..." The thin-faced man looks him up and down for a second time. "Oh. Well, this is awkward."

There is another voice, loud and booming, from within the shed. "Hurry up, it's your turn. Who is it?" the voice demands.

"It's, um, a big skeleton thing," the thin-faced man says, "says he's Death."

From inside the shed, there is silence, and then a muttering, and then, more clearly. "Tell him we've got one."

The thin-faced man turns back to him and smiles

apologetically. "Sorry," he says, "we've already got one."

And then, quietly but firmly, he closes the door.

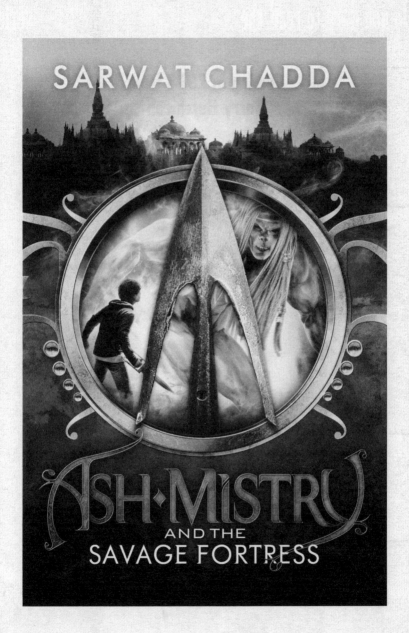

SARWAT CHADDA

ASH·MISTRY
AND THE
SAVAGE FORTRESS

Coming in 2013 from
Barry Hutchison

THE LOST BOOK OF
EVERYTHING

An Afterworlds novel